*Mystery of the Pirate's Ghost*

# MYSTERY OF THE PIRATE'S GHOST

## by *Elizabeth Honness*

*Illustrated by Beth & Joe Krush*

### J. B. Lippincott Company

PHILADELPHIA AND NEW YORK

THE AUTHOR wishes to express her appreciation to the New Haven Colony Historical Society and to Mrs. M. J. Kelley, Custodian of the Old Morris House, Morris Cove, New Haven, Connecticut, for her kindness in opening the house for inspection during the time it is normally closed. Though this house of history inspired the story on these pages, the author has taken liberties with its location and the happenings of the plot are pure invention.

*For Macko*

# Contents

# ❦ 1 ❧

# The Letter That Changed Everything

ALL HAD BEEN much as usual that warm June Saturday morning in the Hubbard house. Abby was upstairs in her room studying for her final math exam. Kit was out in the rear yard batting a tennis ball against the fence. Mrs. Hubbard had just finished making orange sherbet for supper when Mr. Hubbard came home with the mail. Then, everything was changed.

Abby did not expect any letters, but she was tired of studying. She pushed her glossy, straight fair hair back from her warm face and wiped the beads of perspiration from her short upper lip. She closed her book and went downstairs.

"Hi, Dad," she called. "Anything for me?"

"Nothing for you, Pumpkin. I guess you don't rate. But

there's something for Mother. Looks as though the law were after her. She has an impressive looking letter from a lawyer in Boston."

Mrs. Hubbard had come from the kitchen, wiping her hands on her apron. She looked young for her age, thirty-seven. She had dark brown wavy hair, cut short, which fitted her small proud head like a cap. Her cheeks were flushed and her wide-set green eyes were alert with interest.

"A lawyer writing to me, Paul?" She held out her hand for the letter.

"Let me slit the envelope first," said Mr. Hubbard, reaching for the silver paper cutter. He detested having letters ripped opened with thumb or finger so that the envelope was all rumpled.

The letter had two pages. Natalie Hubbard read it to herself with gasps of astonishment. When she had finished she looked dazed.

"What is it? What is it?" asked Mr. Hubbard and Abby.

"Something so incredible I can't believe it!" She handed the letter to her husband. "Here, Paul. Read it! Abby, call Kit. I want Dad to read it to both of you. It concerns the whole family."

Abby ran to the open dining-room window which over-looked the yard. "Hey, Kit," she called. "Come into the house right away. Mommy has an important letter from a lawyer. She wants you to hear it."

Kit was ten, one year younger than Abby. He came bounding into the house, rattling the pots and pans in the kitchen as he passed through. His eyes looked very blue in his tanned round face. His wheat-colored hair was

brushed back from a cowlick and curled in spite of frequent dampenings and brushings.

"What've you done, Ma, to fall afoul the law?" he
asked, flopping down on the couch and throwing his legs
over its arm, thereby endangering a lamp on the end table.

"Watch it, Kit," his mother cautioned. "You'll never
guess in the wide world. Now, Paul, read! I won't believe
it myself until I hear you read the words."

Mr. Hubbard looked at them over the top of his horn-
rimmed glasses. His eyebrows were raised so high deep
furrows creased his forehead. "Hold on to your seats," he
said. "This is a letter from a firm of Boston lawyers called
Follingsbee, Follingsbee, and Thorp. It is addressed to

Mrs. Natalie Pingree Hubbard, 7 Elbow Lane, Tupper-town, Pennsylvania. It begins:

"Dear Madam:

This is to inform you that, under the last will and testament of your late half brother, Jonathan Pingree, who died in Boston on May the fifth of this year, you are sole heir to the old Pingree mansion on Pingree Point, together with such pieces of family furniture that remain in the house, subject to the wishes of his sister, Miss Ann Pingree who may choose what she desires from among the furnishings."

Abby's and Kit's mouths opened into wide O's. "Wow and zowie! A house! Oh boy, oh boy!" shouted Kit.

"A *mansion*, he says!" Abby's voice was hushed. "Mommy, you never told us you had a half brother!"

"I know," said Mrs. Hubbard. "I'd almost forgotten that I did have one, or a half sister, either, for that matter. I'll tell you what little I know about them when Dad finishes the letter. There's more."

Mr. Hubbard stretched his long legs and leaned back in the big wing chair. "Yes, there's more. Suppose you contain yourselves until I finish. Then we'll have a free-for-all of questions. I have a few to ask myself."

He resumed reading:

"The will further provides that a sum be set aside to pay taxes on the property for the next ten years with the stipulation that you occupy the house. In the event that for any personal reasons you decline this inheritance, the property is to be deeded to the State. Furthermore, if at any future time you, or your direct descendants, fail to occupy and maintain the house as a residence, it is to revert to the State as provided in the preceding clause.

"The income from the balance of the estate is left to Miss Ann Pingree during her lifetime. At her death the principal, which is now in excess of $300,-000 is to go to State University after bequests of $10,000 each have been set aside in trust for the surviving children of Natalie and Paul Hubbard."

"Golly day, that's us!" gasped Abby, her eyes, so like her mother's, were round with astonishment.

"Sh-sh!" Kit shushed her.

Mr. Hubbard continued:

"These bequests, too, are contingent upon the Hubbard family living in the house.

"We wish to congratulate you on this fine legacy and to tell you that the house is ready for your occupancy at any time after the necessary papers have been signed. Miss Ann Pingree, who had lived there all of her life, until last year, is now established in an apartment in the nearby town of Thetford, taking with her such furnishings as she could use. The remainder, including many fine pieces dating from the early days of this country, are yours.

"There are certain documents that await your signature and we would appreciate your calling at our Boston office at your earliest convenience. Will you kindly let us know what day and time would suit you? In the meantime, please believe that we are most ready and eager to serve your interests in any legal capacity that may be required.

> "Yours most sincerely,
> Arthur Follingsbee."

Mr. Hubbard folded the letter and inserted it into its envelope. The crackle of paper sounded sharp and loud in the silence that followed his reading.

Mrs. Hubbard's eyes were bright. Abby thought she looked as though she wanted to cry.

Kit was the first to speak. "We'll have to move!" he said. He thought a minute. "Who cares?" he asked. "Whee! Ten thousand dollars for Abby and me!"

Abby was not able to adjust quite so quickly. She had lived in Tuppertown all of her life. Her friends were here, her school. She wasn't sure she wanted to move. "What about Dad's job?" she asked hesitantly. Kit and this old half brother had not seemed to think Dad's work was important.

"Ever since I read the letter for the first time to myself I've been thinking about that," said Mr. Hubbard. "I don't believe my job need stand in the way. I am sure— almost sure, that is, that my firm could arrange a transfer to their New England plant. We have a branch, a big one, not too far from Pingree Point. But if not, it should not be too hard to connect with some other firm in that area. Electrical engineers are in great demand."

He turned to Mrs. Hubbard. "How do you feel about it, Nat? It is really up to you. Though aside from in-heriting a house none of us has ever seen and are not sure we want to live in, it would seem foolish to me to turn down bequests for Abby and Kit. That money would see them both comfortably through college."

"Oh, I agree! Of course I agree one hundred per cent!" said Mrs. Hubbard. "And I feel certain we'll like the house. None of you can possibly know what it means to me to inherit it. To have a half brother remember me, a brother I never met in all my life!"

"Tell us about him," pleaded Abby. "Tell us all you know about this other family."

"I'll try," said Mrs. Hubbard. "But you must remember that what little I know I heard from my mother and she died when I was just your age, Abby. That was a long time ago." She rested her head against the back of her chair and sighed deeply, then fanned herself with her handkerchief. "Before I begin, I think we all need a long cool drink. There's some frozen lemonade in the icebox. Suppose you fix it, Abby. I'm just too overcome by all this to budge. Get a plate of cookies, too, will you, Kit? You know where to find them."

## ❧ 2 ❧

# The Half Relations

NATALIE HUBBARD SIPPED gratefully from the tall iced glass before she began her story. Abby and Kit, the plate of cookies between them, curled up on the couch.

"We're all ears, Ma," said Kit between bites of cookie.

"We knew you were an orphan," said Abby, "but you never told us you had a half brother and sister."

"Well," began Mrs. Hubbard. "You know my father died when I was very young, so young I have no memory of him at all. He was named Nathaniel Pingree. My name, Natalie, was the nearest to Nathaniel my mother could find for a girl. He was old when my mother married him, sixty and a widower. His first marriage had been extremely unhappy, Mother told me. He stuck it out as long as he could, but when his children were in their teens, he made over the house and most of his property to his wife in trust for his children and came to Philadelphia to start a new life. I don't know any of the circumstances that caused the break-up of the first marriage.

"Years later, after his wife had died, he met my mother who was working as a secretary in an office where he was a frequent business caller. She was half his age, but they fell in love and were married. They had only four happy years together before he died suddenly of a heart attack when I was two."

"How awful never to have known your father," said Abby. She threw a loving glance at her own dad who sat hunched in the wing chair his gaze fixed upon his wife.

"Yes, it was hard," said Mrs. Hubbard. "I often wondered about him. My mother kept his photograph on her bureau. He didn't begin to look his age. He had all his hair," she grinned at Mr. Hubbard whose hairline was already receding. "He had dark eyes and a sensitive face. I know he liked to play bridge, and he loved books. My mother said I resembled him. She never talked about his previous marriage. She didn't like to think about it or remember it, I suppose."

"Was it after he died that you went to live with Great-Aunt Sophie?" Kit asked.

Mrs. Hubbard nodded. "My Aunt Sophie had plenty of room for us in her house. She was a lot older than Mother and lived on in their parents' house after their death. She taught school and so was home fairly early in the afternoons and could help keep an eye on me. As soon as I was old enough to go to nursery school my mother went back to business. My father had left some insurance money which she saved to finance my college education.

There was nothing else except what little cash he had in the bank at the time of his death, so you see she had to go back to work. Aunt Sophie was awfully good to us. When my own mother died ten years later, she was like a second mother to me."

"You haven't told us about your half relations!" Abby reminded her mother. She had an inner picture of half a brother, split right down the middle, and half a sister, the top half floating in space. It was so odd a picture she giggled.

"What's funny?" asked Kit.

When she explained, her parents laughed, too.

"I'm sure they were able-bodied and whole," said Mrs. Hubbard. "Mother told me that my father had another grown-up son and daughter and that the old Pingree place in New England belonged to them. She explained to me that they were 'half' brother and sister because we had the same father but different mothers. Jonathan was close to forty when I was born! More than old enough to have been my father! His sister Ann was two years younger. She must be well into her seventies now.

"They never made any effort to get to know my mother or me. I know that Mother always resented the fact that her husband's children by his first marriage totally ignored her. Not that I ever heard her mention this. I was so young I wouldn't have understood. But later Aunt Sophie told me. And for my mother's sake, I couldn't help feeling a bit hurt, too. That is why I am so completely flabbergasted at being remembered in Jonathan's will."

"What do you suppose struck the old fellow?" Mr. Hubbard wondered aloud. "What could have made him suddenly decide to leave you the house and make those bequests to our children?"

"I can only guess," said Mrs. Hubbard. She finished her lemonade and set the glass on a coaster on the low table near her chair. "He apparently never married. Nor did Ann. She is referred to as Miss Pingree in the lawyer's letter, remember?

"That means that I am the only blood relative either of them had on the Pingree side of the family. I know from what my mother told me that my father was very proud of his family forebears and that he had a deep love for the old home place. Maybe my half brother felt it was only right and just that the home should come to me. I am the only Pingree left and perhaps he wanted my children to live there."

"Could be," said Mr. Hubbard. "I still can't get used to the idea, though. How did he know your married name?"

"Aunt Sophie sent him an announcement when we were married. He did not acknowledge it in any way or send a present. I hadn't expected him to and so thought nothing of it, but she was offended. I pointed out to her that those two, Jonathan and Ann, probably took their mother's side in whatever the trouble was between her and our father. Also they may not have liked the idea of him marrying a woman so much younger than himself. At any rate, I can understand better now. They had no real responsibility for me so why should they concern themselves with my existence?"

"It's going to take a lot of getting used to," said Abby, letting her gaze drift around the familiar room. This morning, before the letter arrived, seemed long ago. Now everything was different—their whole lives would be changed. She tried to imagine herself and their furniture in a strange setting. It made her feel queer and a bit forlorn, even though she was terribly excited over this extraordinary thing that was happening to them.

Kit was getting restless. He stretched himself and arose from the couch. "Guess I'll try to get a game of tennis," he said.

"Good idea," said his father. "But don't spill any of this to your friends yet. Let's keep it in the family until we know more about our plans."

# The Inherited House

IN SPITE OF their inner turmoil, Abby and Kit passed their final exams satisfactorily and were promoted into the seventh and sixth grades respectively. They had a sinking feeling when they realized that they would not be returning to their old school in September.

In the meantime, Mr. Hubbard had had a conference with his superiors at the plant. He was congratulated on the family's good fortune and was told that a transfer could probably be arranged to the New England branch. He was also advised to take a week of his vacation as soon as the children's exams were over so that the whole family could drive to Boston to see the lawyer and inspect the house.

Mrs. Hubbard telephoned for an appointment. It was

set up for the Monday after school closed. Early on Sunday morning they were on their way.

Abby and Kit never did remember much about the Boston part of their trip although staying in a large city hotel was a new experience for them. Abby felt as though a spell had been cast upon them. They moved, they talked, they ate their meals, they saw new sights, but a veil hung between them and reality. It was as though two robots had replaced herself and Kit. They did not begin to come to life until after their father and mother had emerged from Mr. Follingsbee's office and their father informed them, "The papers are all signed and sealed and the house is ours."

Soon after they were in the car and driving out of the city toward Pingree Point. That was when Abby and Kit came out of their dream state.

"How long will it take? When will we get there?" Kit wanted to know.

"We'll have to stop for some lunch, but we ought to be there by two," said Mr. Hubbard. "Mr. Follingsbee telephoned Miss Pingree and asked her to meet us there at that time."

Mr. Follingsbee's directions had been explicit. They left the New England Throughway at the proper exit, drove along several residential streets in the village of Thetford, then turned on to Shipspar Lane which led to Pingree Point. At several bends in the road, where the trees gave way to open meadows, they glimpsed blue water.

"Look! There's the ocean!" cried Abby. "I can smell it!"

"Silly, that's not the ocean. It's the river, the Quinnibec. It flows into Long Island Sound here," said Kit. He had been studying the road map and showed Abby where they were.

"The tide comes further up than this," said Mr. Hubbard, "so you do smell the sea."

The car had begun to climb a barely perceptible grade, past houses set well back from the road. Then the road ended at a driveway. A car parked under a shade tree undoubtedly belonged to Miss Pingree. They hardly spared it a glance because their house stood before them. It could be none other, for it was the last house on the road, old and massive and weather-worn, but welcoming beneath its tall oak trees. Beyond its sweep of lawn, beyond the white picket fence, the land dropped off and there was only blueness of sky and sea.

Stone chimneys rose from either end of the central portion of the house which was two stories high with an attic under its steep-pitched roof. The front was white clapboard with many small-paned windows. At the left, on the east, a large ell of stone and clapboard extended to the rear. An enormous lilac, growing in an angle·of the house, perfumed the air with sweetness. Dark green shrubs were massed at either side of the paneled front door.

As the Hubbard family approached, the door opened and a slight erect figure was framed against the darkness of the hall, Miss Ann Pingree. Her short hair was white and curly in a soft fluff around her head. Like a dandelion gone to seed Abby said to herself. She wondered what would happen if she blew a big puff of wind at her new aunt, whose eyes were bright and intensely blue in a face that was finely chiseled and etched with tiny lines.

Miss Pingree stepped toward them holding out both

hands. "You must be the Hubbards," she said in a soft
voice. "And you are my sister Natalie." She went directly
to Mrs. Hubbard and looked at her long and intently. "Yes,
I can see my father in you," she said. "After all these years
of not knowing each other I can't bear just to shake hands.
Would you mind kissing me? And then please introduce
me to the rest of the family."

Natalie Hubbard bent down and kissed Miss Pingree
gently on the cheek and the old lady put her arms around
her for a moment. Then she took a handkerchief from her
suit pocket and blew her nose. Abby saw that her eyes
were brighter than before.

"This is my husband Paul," said Mrs. Hubbard hastily.
"And the children are Abby and Kit."

Miss Pingree shook hands with each of them. Her hands were little and bony with soft wrinkled skin.

"You must forgive me if I seem a bit excited," she said. "It isn't every day an old lady acquires a niece and nephew and meets a sister for the first time." She turned to Mr. Hubbard. "I don't mean to leave you out, Paul! I am very happy to have a new brother, too. I've been lonely without one since Jonathan's been gone."

She gave Natalie Hubbard another long look. "You've probably been wondering why I made no effort to get to know you before," she said. "I'd be wondering that if I were in your shoes. But you see, I never even knew you existed until Jonathan received your wedding announce-

ment. Then we both thought it would seem rather intrusive to suddenly make ourselves known to you. But we talked it over and decided together that we wanted you to inherit this house. We felt that after we are gone we wanted it to belong to someone with Pingree blood in her veins."

"I think I understand," said Natalie Hubbard. "And I'm very grateful. But I'm still in a state of shock. I keep feeling I shall wake up and realize all this has been happening in a novel I've been reading, and not to me."

"Give yourself a good pinch," said Miss Pingree. "It's all true. Abby and Kit, I want you to call me Aunt Ann. Start right away! That's the thing I have to pinch myself about. I never dreamed that I'd have the experience of being an aunt, and I'm tickled pink!"

Kit gave her a big grin. "Aunt Ann . . . I like the way it sounds," he said. "The house is awful big, Aunt Ann. When are we going inside?"

Aunt Ann gave a tiny chuckle. "Well, right away, my boy. Right this very minute. Just follow me." She led the way into the house.

# ⤜ 4 ⤛

# Some Family History

AFTER THE BRIGHT SUNLIGHT outside and the heat, the house seemed dim and cool. They were in a long center hall with wide floor boards and a staircase rising at the left.

"This is the oldest part of the house," said Aunt Ann. "It was built in 1690 by the first Pingree to come to America. The frame is of white oak and the end walls of this central part are of granite, quarried right here on the land. They had to make do with what they had in those days. They even made the mortar out of ground-up oyster shells and sand from the beach."

"Golly," said Kit, "and it's stood all these years!"

"Yes, they built to last then," said Aunt Ann. "And this lasted until the Revolutionary War when the British burned it in 1779. But stone won't burn and the floor and some of the original beams escaped damage and the end walls with their chimneys still stood. So the grandson of the first Jonathan Pingree rebuilt it and remodeled it, too. The only thing the British missed burning was a farm shed. Jonathan had it moved against the west wall, and he and his family lived there while the house was being re-built. When they moved back into the main house, the shed became the kitchen. Later on the second floor was added to it and the whole section was extended several feet to the rear so it could be entered from the main part of the house. A later Pingree who had a big family added the ell on the east where the dining room is. So you see the house has grown with the years."

Mr. Hubbard had been examining the ironwork on the doors. "These are hand-forged, they must be." He indicated the huge H and L shaped hinges.

Aunt Ann nodded her fluffy head. "They are indeed. And the framework of this old part is put together with wooden pegs instead of nails. Come, you must see the rooms. This one on the left is the library. Lots of books still on the shelves, you see. And a fireplace to have a jolly blaze on a cold night. I hope you'll want to keep that secretary, Natalie." She indicated a tall desk with solid doors of pine.

Mrs. Hubbard went over to it and ran her hand down the satiny wood. "Do I want to keep it!" she exclaimed. "It is gorgeous! May I look inside?" Without waiting for an answer she pulled the tall doors open, revealing upright partitions and shelves and little drawers and pigeonholes. "How can you possibly not want it for yourself?"

"I have a desk, an old one, too, but one that fits better

into my smaller quarters. If you hadn't appreciated this one, I would have been terribly disappointed in you!"

Natalie Hubbard gave Miss Pingree a hug. "It's the desk I've been longing for! It will be so wonderful to have enough room for our books, too. We've never had a library, and this room surpasses any I could wish for."

The rest of the first floor was nearly as wonderful. There was a long living room on the other side of the center hall with two fireplaces. Abby noticed that the andirons were still there and that fire tongs and a shovel stood in a holder on each hearth. There were wing chairs and a Queen Anne sofa in this room and a tall highboy which Miss Pingree said she had no use for. *Lucky us,* thought Abby. *We wouldn't have enough furniture of our own for both a library and a living room.*

Miss Pingree led them through a passage from that room to a sturdy door. "Help me unbar this, it's hard to do," she said to Mr. Hubbard. "We don't use this room but I want you to see it."

The bar was stiff, but Mr. Hubbard finally released it from its brackets. Miss Pingree entered the room first and slid open the shutters from several of its small-paned windows. They saw that the room was enormous with a huge fireplace and massive dark beams supporting the ceiling.

"It is hard to think of this ever being a farm shed," said Miss Pingree. "See that wall oven in the back of the fireplace? They baked their bread there. And this is where they washed dishes." She indicated a stone sink set into a recess with an opening through the wall where waste water could run out.

"No, Abby, they could not turn faucets on for water in
those days. It had to be drawn from the well and carried
here in buckets. We always kept this room closed off from
the rest of the house. There's no basement under it so it
has only the fireplace for heat in the winter. We had more
than enough living space without it. But it was a handy
place to store things."

The Hubbards followed Miss Pingree back the way they
had come, across the center hall, through a passage to the
rear of the library that led into the southeast ell, and
entered a large sunny room with a fireplace at the far end.

"This is the dining room," said Miss Pingree unneces-
sarily.

A long trestle table stood in the center of the room and a pine hutch for dishes was against one wall. There were ten Windsor chairs. Abby and her mother exchanged a glance of pure delight. Now they could get rid of that old shabby table and chairs they had used so long at home.

"You can see my herb garden through the windows here," said Miss Pingree. There was gentle pride in her voice as she showed them the neatly planted beds. "I used to take care of it myself, but it has been too much for me the last few years. John, who drives for me, is a good gardener and he has taken it over. He lives with his wife, Essie, in that little house which is attached to the end of the ell, between it and the barn, and he has taken care of the house for me, too, since I moved out a year ago. He's been invaluable. I hope you will let him go on living there. He would be glad to do work for you in return, I'm sure. I only use him in the afternoons. And Essie is a marvelous cleaner."

This was something Mr. Follingsbee had failed to mention.

"That sounds great," said Mr. Hubbard. "If you vouch for him I'm sure we'll have no objections. I wouldn't feel that we could afford to hire a handy man very often, but if he and his wife are willing to swap work now and then in exchange for staying on, I think we can make some arrangement satisfactory to us both. Don't you think so, Nat?"

"I was wondering how I'd ever find anyone to help me clean," said Mrs. Hubbard beaming. "This sounds perfect. Of course he can stay, as far as I'm concerned."

"Good," said Miss Pingree. "He'll be glad not to have to move. Now you must see the kitchen."

They followed her into another large sunny room with an enormous fireplace. "You could roast an ox in that!" said Mr. Hubbard.

Abby glanced anxiously about. She could not imagine her mother cooking in that fireplace. She was relieved to see an electric stove along the opposite wall and a modern stainless steel sink set into a gleaming counter. There were cupboards above and beyond them a large refrigerator.

"The only thing lacking is an electric dishwasher," said Mother after she had inspected cupboards and shelves approvingly. "I would like to have one installed under the counter next to the sink."

"We'll attend to that tomorrow," said Mr. Hubbard.

Kit nudged Abby and puckered up his lips in a silent whistle. Dad was certainly letting himself go. But almost at once he realized that when they sold their house at home there'd be extra cash for improvements on this one.

Miss Pingree was answering Dad's questions about the furnace. It was a fairly new oil burner, they learned. The radiators were concealed behind wooden grilles. "You won't have any trouble keeping warm," she told them.

"Good gracious!" exclaimed Mrs. Hubbard, glancing at her watch. "It's four-thirty already. I had no idea it had gotten that late. You must be tired, Ann. We shouldn't have kept you on your feet so long."

"We've taken enough of your time. We ought to be checking in at the motel," Mr. Hubbard said. "We want to start home tomorrow as soon as I've arranged about the dishwasher."

"But we haven't been upstairs yet!" cried Abby. "I have to choose my room."

"Of course you do," said Aunt Ann. "You just run on upstairs and look around by yourselves. I'll rest a bit down here. I confess my legs don't hold me up quite so long or so well as they used to."

# ❦ 5 ❧

# The Pirate's Ghost

THEY MADE A QUICK INSPECTION of the upstairs rooms. There were six bedrooms, four in the main house, the other two in the ell. All had fireplaces and some were furnished with fourposter beds with canopy tops. There were also several highboys and old chests and some candlestands and firescreens which made Abby and Mrs. Hubbard exclaim with joy.

Abby had no trouble in deciding which room she wanted—a rear one, not too large, overlooking the blue waters of the Sound. It had built-in cupboards for clothes and two deep-recessed windows.

Kit plunked for the room in front of Abby's without a bed. He said he preferred to sleep in his own, the one he was used to, and he didn't want any fancy net ceiling over the top of it, either!

There were two bathrooms, large and fairly modern. "These must have been dressing rooms, once," said Mrs. Hubbard. "Nobody has bathrooms this big today." She was pleased to find plenty of shelves for linens in the bathroom closets.

Kit had been exploring. He had come on a passageway identical to the one on the first floor leading into the great unused old kitchen. He opened a door at the end and shouted, "Look what I've found! This room is large enough to give a party in!"

They hurried to join him. The room was long with a vaulted ceiling and many windows. It had a polished floor and seats built along the sides. At the south end was a small room with a window opening through its wall into the larger room. "I believe Kit is right," said Mrs. Hubbard. "It looks to me as though this room had been a ballroom!"

When they came downstairs, Miss Pingree told them that it was indeed a ballroom. "But we never used it," she added. "We kept this whole section closed off."

"Imagine having a ballroom of our own!" Abby's eyes shone.

"That little room at the far end was called a retiring room. That is where the chaperones sat to keep an eye on the dancers. There's a narrow stairway that leads down to the kitchen below so refreshments could be brought up."

"Well," said Mr. Hubbard. "I suppose a ballroom might come in handy. We could set up our Ping-pong table there, and you kids could even rollerskate on that slick floor on a rainy day."

Natalie Hubbard gave her sister a quick glance to see how she reacted to this. But Miss Pingree only smiled. "Use it any way you choose," she said. "It's your house now. Though I think the ghosts of those elegant ladies and gentlemen would shake their heads sadly if they saw the outlandish way young people dance today." She cocked her head at Abby and Kit. "That reminds me! I mean the ghosts do. There are one or two things I forgot to tell you about the house. There's supposed to be a real ghost here, though I myself have never seen him."

"Really!" Mrs. Hubbard was startled.

"Oh, tell us about him," begged Abby.

"I will some day. There is another legend, too, about the smugglers' tunnel."

"Honest Injun?" said Kit, not trusting his ears.

"Don't get too excited," cautioned his aunt. "It's never been found. I don't believe, really, that it ever existed. But the legend says that a tunnel once led from the basement to the shore and that smugglers used it to bring in contraband."

"Contraband!" echoed Kit.

"Yes, sugar and molasses and such from the Indies. That was after Great Britain imposed high taxes on the colonies and would not let them trade with any country but England."

The old lady looked at Abby's and Kit's open mouths with amusement. "You'd better close your traps or you'll catch flies," she said.

This was so unexpected that both children giggled.

"Oh, yes, there's one thing more," she said, obviously enjoying the sensation she was creating. "Behind one of the fireplaces upstairs there's a secret closet that I'll show you sometime. It's a place where the children of the family could hide during Indian raids."

She refused to tell them anything more. "We'll have lots of time when you come here to live," she said. "But I'm tired now."

She waited for them to precede her out the front door, took a large key from her handbag and locked it, and then walked with them to their car. "Here," she said to Natalie Hubbard. "Take this. The key is yours now. If there is anything I can do to help before you move in, let me know. Just Thetford, will reach me when you know what date you will arrive. And now come and meet John. I know it will be a load off his mind when you tell him he can stay."

John got out of the car as he saw them approaching and stood, cap in hand. He was a short, squarish man with a bald head, plump rosy cheeks and little eyes that peered out from under bushy brows and darted from one to the other of the Hubbards.

"John, this is my new family," said Miss Pingree. "My sister, Mrs. Hubbard, her husband, and Abby and Kit."

John bobbed his head at Mrs. Hubbard, shook Mr. Hubbard's hand. "I'm glad to meet you," he said. "It's mighty nice for Miss Pingree to have a family again. The house won't be so lonely having some young ones in it."

He quirked an eyebrow at Kit and Abby and smiled.

"We hope you'll stay on," said Mr. Hubbard. "Miss Pingree suggested you might be willing to take care of the yard and garden for me instead of paying rent and I'd consider that a fair exchange if it's okay by you."

John smiled with more warmth than before. "It sure is! More than fair! The wife will be happy we don't have to move. Miss Pingree'll tell you she's a handy one with a mop and broom."

"I already have," said Aunt Ann. "Good, then everything is settled to everybody's satisfaction. Now, John, take me home."

She blew a kiss to the Hubbards as her car drove off.

# ❦ 6 ❦

# New Friends

"WHERE AM I?" Abby wondered as she awoke on an August Tuesday morning the day after they had moved. Her eyes took in the net canopy overhead with its pleated flounce of ruffles between the tall posts of the bed. "This isn't my bed," she thought.

She sniffed the air flooding in at the window. It smelled brisk and clean with a hint of saltiness unfamiliar to her. Long fingers of sunlight reached across the wide floor boards, touching the heap of clothes she had stepped out of last night—blue shorts and jersey, underwear and faded blue sneakers.

Then, realization came. This was home after all—their new-old home on Pingree Point. She bounded out of bed and ran to the window. Yes, there was the sea! Beyond the sweep of lawn, beyond the drop-off of the bluff on which the house stood, stretched a vast blueness. The muted mewing of sea gulls came to her ears. She could see their arcing flight and their sudden arrowing dives into the sea before they reappeared with breakfast in their beaks.

That smudge of smoke on the horizon must belong to a freighter or some big ship on its way to Boston. The sky was clear and blue above, with only puffs of cloud. The sun glittered on the water and on dewy cobwebs spangling the grass.

Abby drew a deep breath. How good the sea air smelled! She filled her lungs again and let the air out slowly in a sigh of delight. "We're here! We're really here!" she exulted.

The weeks just past seemed far away. Dad's firm had found a place for him in the New England branch and he had gone on ahead to begin work there, but had taken the second week of his vacation for the final packing up and moving. There had been days of sorting and choosing what they would bring, and disposing of things that would no longer be needed, such as beds and old dining room furniture and chairs. There were good-bys to friends, promises to write and to come back to visit, farewell parties. There were processions of people come to inspect their old home before it was finally sold. And then, yesterday, the long drive to Pingree Point, the wait for the moving van, and the excitement of deciding where things should go and getting unpacked and halfway settled. They had not accepted Aunt Ann's invitation to have supper with her— there had been too much to do right here. Instead they had had a pick-up supper in the kitchen after Mother had made a hurried trip to Thetford to lay in supplies.

Aunt Ann had understood and had promised to drop in on them today. The whole family was eager to see her again. Abby and Kit especially wanted to hear what she could tell them about the ghost, and also to be shown the secret closet.

Abby looked around her new room with pleased satisfaction. She had unpacked all her clothes and books last night. The only thing lacking was curtains for the two windows. Mother had promised to let her choose the material to make them herself. She thought she might buy a percale sheet with dainty sprigs of flowers on it and cut that up for curtains.

She took clean underwear from a drawer and began to dress. Apparently she was the first one up. Her watch told her it was seven-thirty but she could hear no sounds of anyone stirring. However, when she entered the kitchen, she found Kit already at the breakfast table.

"I might have known it!" she said. A box of Rice Krispies stood by an empty cereal dish and Kit was busily stuffing his face with egg and toast. "How many eggs? Three? Oh, Kit, you do eat like a horse."

"I can't help it if I'm hungry. It's the sea air," Kit looked injured. "At least I get up and fix my own breakfast without bothering anybody."

"Yes, I'll hand you that. But sea air!" Abby snorted. "That's no excuse. You ate just as much without sea air at home."

"Well, this is home now, and I've a perfect right to eat as much as I need. Stop picking on me."

"Oh, all right." Abby filled a bowl with cereal and poured herself a glass of juice. "It's a good thing we have a dishwasher, with all that china still to be unpacked and washed. Let's hurry outdoors before Mommy starts us working. I want to see the beach."

"So do I," said Kit, getting up to take his dishes to the sink. That was another commendable thing about Kit. He cleaned up after himself.

Abby took a final gulp of milk and joined him with her bowl and glasses. "We'll do them when we get back," she said. "I can't believe we have a place to swim right here without having to go to a public pool like we did in Tuppertown."

They went out the kitchen door. John was on his knees weeding in the pungent-smelling herb garden beside the house. He looked up as they came near. "You're early birds," he said. "Going to explore, I'll bet."

"We want to see the beach," said Kit.

"The way down is over there across the driveway and through the gate in the fence. Mind the steps. They're steep."

"Thanks," said Abby. She glanced back as they came to the gate. John had risen from his weeding and was standing watching them.

Once down the steep stone steps fitted into the side of the bluff, they kicked off their sneakers and wiggled their toes in the sand. Then they looked back the way they had come. The bluff rose abruptly from the beach. Shrubs and vines covered it, growing between outcroppings of rock. The beach curved into a shallow cove and then continued. Further on they could see shingled cottages and summer houses spaced rather closely and wondered if any of them contained children their age.

"I'll race you!" cried Kit. And at once both children were running barefoot up the beach, skirting the edges of little waves which sent creamy lines of foam to form scallops on the sand. Schools of sandpipers took wing at their approach. Ahead, they could see other sandpipers scurrying after the receding waves, then teetering on their slender legs as they snapped up whatever appetizing food the sea left behind.

"Isn't this fun!" cried Abby, pausing for breath. She flung her arms toward sea and sky. "The sandpipers chase the waves and then the waves chase them!"

"Maybe they're afraid to get their feet wet!"

"It looks that way. They're catching sand fleas. There's a flea hiding wherever you see those little air bubbles in the wet sand."

Abby and Kit were unaware they were no longer alone. They whirled around at the sound of a voice saying, "Hi! Are you the kids who just moved into the old Pingree house? You must be 'cause we haven't seen you around before. Didn't mean to startle you. My name's Chuck Burgess and this gal here is my next-door neighbor, Patty Brown. We live in two of those cottages you can see from here."

"We were hoping there'd be some children around," said Abby. "This is my brother, Kit, and I'm Abby Hubbard. We've only been here since last night and this is our first chance to explore. It's a neat beach."

Chuck must be about her age, she decided. He was brown from the sun. His eyes were a light clear gray and he had a short blunt nose above a mouth that curled up at the corners. Patty was younger. Her skin was olive-toned. Her dark hair was tangled from the wind and her brown eyes were friendly under ruffled bangs.

"You were watching the sandpipers," she said. "Did you notice what funny marks they make in the sand? My mother says their tracks look like featherstitching."

"Why she's right! They do! Featherstitching on the sand." The idea amused Abby.

"You must be related to the Pingrees or something," said Chuck. "We never thought old Miss Pingree would let anyone else live in her house. Have you seen the ghost yet?"

"If there really is a ghost!" said Abby. "There seems to be quite a bit of doubt about it. Miss Pingree is our aunt, our mother's half sister. Her brother left the house to us in his will."

"Yes, and she's going to tell us about the ghost when she comes today," said Kit.

"Is that a fact? I hope you'll let us in on what she says."

"Maybe we will and maybe we won't. It all depends."

"On what?" asked Patty.

"On whether it's private family business or not," said Kit.

Chuck winked at Abby over Kit's head. They both found Kit's self-importance funny.

"Come off it, Kit," said Abby. "A ghost is a matter of general interest. Did you two ever see it or hear of anyone who did?"

"No-o-o," Patty was hesitant. "Once Chuck thought he saw some faint lights wink on and off in the end of the house opposite the wing. That was after Miss Pingree moved out. It made us wonder."

"That's the part of the house that's never used," exclaimed Abby. "I can't imagine why any lights would be there."

"How do you get along with John?" Chuck asked suddenly. It was such an abrupt change of subject it surprised Kit and Abby.

"All right so far. He seems friendly enough and pleased to have a family live here again. I know he's glad not to have to move. Why do you ask?" Abby showed her puzzlement.

"Oh, I just wondered," said Chuck. "He always chases any kids away who come near the place. See those 'No Trespassing' signs on the stakes over there by the bluff? He doesn't even want us to come here to swim. And it's the best beach anywhere around."

"Maybe he's just putting on an act for us," said Kit. "But that would be a kind of funny thing to do."

Just then Mrs. Hubbard's voice hailed them from the top of the bluff. "Abby, Kit, I need you," she called.

"We've got to go," said Abby regretfully. "But come back for a swim this afternoon. John has nothing to say about who swims here now."

"We'd love to, at least I would," said Patty.

"Me, too," Chuck grinned, showing very white teeth. "Three o'clock okay? The tide will be right then."

# ❦ 7 ❦

# "A Pirate in Spite of Himself"

THEY HAD a wonderful swim. The sea was calm and smooth as satin. Abby and Chuck swam abreast far out from the shore, then turned and floated in the gentle swell, rising and falling with its motion. *The cradle of the deep,* Abby thought, enjoying the sun's warmth on her face. Her body felt light and weightless as though it could not possibly sink, the water was so buoyant. Far out on the horizon sails dipped and hovered like white butterflies on the blue expanse of sea. There was no sound but the distant drone of passing motor boats and the occasional cry of a gull.

"Are there ever any big waves?" she asked Chuck.

"Wait till we have a Northeaster! You'll see some waves then. It won't be a mill pond like this." He turned, dove down under Abby and came up on her other side. "You should have been here when we had our last hurricane. Waves as high as a house, pounding and rampaging, tossing boats up on land, smashing cottages. The damage was awful. But no one got killed. Hurricane warnings came in time."

"Gosh, I'm glad our house is on high ground." She could just see its roof line, shadowed by treetops, above the headland.

Kit was waving and calling. Abby pulled her cap up from one ear. "Come in," he yelled. "Mother said not to swim far out."

"I guess we'd better go back, Chuck."

Abby was a strong swimmer. She had passed Red Cross swimming tests and won her Junior Life Saver's badge, but she knew Mother was right. It wasn't wise to swim too far from shore in strange waters. Chuck synchronized his crawl stroke to hers. Their right arms flashed up and out, their left elbows came out of the water together as their right hands disappeared, their mouths gulped air at the same instant, their feet fluttered up and down as their bodies were propelled toward shore.

"Jeepers!" said Patty admiringly as they came up to her and Kit. "I wish I could swim like that."

Chuck flung his head back to shake the water from his eyes and ears. He gave her a wide grin. "Abby's pretty good and you can be, too, if you just keep at it. Come on, I'll race you. Last man in is a dead duck."

The sea was churned to a froth with their mad scramble to shore. Breathless and laughing they flung themselves down on the warm sand. Kit was last man in. He had slowed down purposely so Patty would not have to be the dead duck. She suspected as much and gave him a smile of thanks.

Abby pulled off her cap and let her hair fall about her face. It glinted gold in the sun. She towelled her arms and legs briskly, then consulted her watch which she had left in her beach bag. "It's nearly four. We'll have to go. Aunt Ann is coming to tell us about the ghost. Say, why don't you come, too, and meet her and our parents? We want them to know you."

"Could we come all wet like this?" Patty asked.

"Sure, that won't matter," said Kit. "We'll be wet, too."

Chuck slung a green towel across his tanned shoulders. "What are we waiting for?" he asked.

Thus Aunt Ann was greeted by four damp young people instead of two.

She was seated in a garden chair at the side of the house in the shade, looking small and dainty beside the long angular figure of Mr. Hubbard stretched out in a deck chair. Mrs. Hubbard, in a fresh cotton dress, was pouring iced tea into glasses.

"You are just in time," she said, after the introductions had been made. "If you children would rather have cokes or root beer you'll find bottles in the refrigerator. Bring some extra glasses, Abby. It is certainly nice for Abby and Kit to find some young friends in the neighborhood. Do you live here the year round?"

"We do and we don't," said Patty. "Our fathers teach at the University and we lived in Haven City most of the year, but we come for weekends lots of times through the year, and of course now we are here for most of the summer."

"Professor Burgess, to be sure," said Aunt Ann. "Of

course I know him. His father used to take me to parties when we were young. If I'd been a bit quicker I'd have recognized you at once as his son, Chuck. Your resemblance to him is striking."

"Poor pop," said Chuck.

"Have some cookies," said Mr. Hubbard. "You must be hungry after your swim. Just help yourselves. Ah, here come Kit and Abby with an assortment of bottles. I hope they remembered the opener."

"You have Aunt Ann to thank for the cookies," said Mrs. Hubbard. "She knew we'd be too busy getting unpacked for me to have time to make any."

"It was my 'welcome home' offering," said Aunt Ann. "I must say you've been busy. The house looks settled already, even though it still lacks curtains. It makes me very happy to see it this way."

"Could you tell us about the ghost now?" asked Kit.

Aunt Ann glanced toward Chuck and Patty who met her gaze with shining expectancy.

"You won't be bored if we talk about ghosts?" she asked them. She did not try to conceal the twinkle in her eyes.

"Gosh, no," said Chuck. "We are perishing to hear about that ghost."

The twinkle became a smile. "Then you'll have to bear with me while I tell a bit of family history because the ghost won't make sense unless I do."

"Fire away," said Mr. Hubbard, tilting his chair forward so he was sitting upright. "We're hungry for more family history."

Aunt Ann put down her glass and sat up straight in her chair, her small feet in their white summer shoes close together on the grass.

"I'll have to start way back with your many times great-grandfather, Abby and Kit. His name was Jonathan Pingree. He came to America in 1688 from England and after a year in Boston he brought his family to what is now Haven City and bought this land on Pingree Point from the Indians. This house was built a year later and he moved in with his wife Prudence and their six children. He wanted to be near the sea as he owned several sailing vessels and from all accounts was a prosperous shipbuilder.

"I wouldn't be surprised if he had not been in the privateering trade. King William the third was at war with France just then and he issued 'Letters of Marque and Reprisal' to seafaring men in the Colonies which entitled them to capture enemy ships and bring them into port. The captor could claim a major part of the ship's cargo, and enormous sums of money were made in this manner."

"Whee! You mean we had an ancestor who was a pirate!" Abby's eyes sparkled. This made family history much more exciting.

Aunt Ann nodded her fluff of a head. "We can't *prove* that Jonathan was one. Privateering was a legitimate affair in those days, but the line between that and piracy was finely drawn."

"Oh, I hope he was!" said Kit. "Go on, please tell us some more."

"There was a pirate in the family even though Jonathan may not have been. His son Robert, his youngest son, was a pirate in spite of himself."

"How could that be?" Chuck asked.

"He went to sea on one of his father's trading ships and the boat was attacked by pirates. This happened quite frequently. All of the older sailors were set adrift in a lifeboat, but Robert and a few other young men were forced to join the pirate crew."

"Wow! You mean a guy could be forced to be a pirate even if he did not want to be?" Kit was indignant. "But how did his family ever find it out?"

"They didn't know what had happened to Robert for a long time," said Aunt Ann. "I suppose they gave the ship up for lost when it did not return. A year or so later, though, one of the sailors who had been set adrift showed up at Pingree Point. He was the only survivor and he told the family what had happened. He'd had a bad time himself from thirst and hunger and was weak and half dead when he was picked up by a whaling ship outward bound. He had to sail halfway around the world before the ship came home to Nantucket with its whale oil cargo.

"Robert was never seen again. His family feared he had died in some pirate fight, or had become so involved in piracy he did not dare show his face. You see, there was a law which made piracy punishable by death. Only if a sailor, newly arrived in port, could prove before a magistrate that he had been forced into piracy, could he escape the death penalty. And, mark this, he also would have to promise to expose his fellow pirates."

"It would take a brave man to do that," said Mr. Hubbard.

Mrs. Hubbard had been listening to her sister with complete attention. "Is he the ghost?" she asked.

Aunt Ann smiled. "You guessed it," she said. "The ghost of Robert, the pirate, tries to come home. He is supposed to appear on windy nights, rapping on doors and windows, begging to be let in."

Abby shuddered. "Did you ever see him?"

"Not I," said Aunt Ann. "But I won't say I haven't heard him. You know that on windy nights you can hear all sorts of sounds, particularly in an old house. After hearing a story like this it is not hard to interpret them as ghostly noises. But don't be frightened, children, if you do hear sounds. Likely as not it will be the stairs creaking, or a tree branch tapping against the walls."

Abby gave another shiver. She wouldn't have admitted it to Kit, but she was sure the first time she heard a strange sound at night she would think it was Robert's ghost.

"Didn't anyone ever see him?" asked Kit.

"Oh, there have been those who said they have. My mother had an Irish maid when we were young, and she swore she saw him one stormy night. She said she looked out of her window and saw a tall man in a long cape with knee britches. He had a bandanna tied around his head and he carried a sea bag, and he limped. She was so scared she wouldn't work for my mother any more and left the next day. But she had a vivid imagination and she had heard that there was supposed to be a pirate's ghost. She did not get along too well with my mother and we thought she probably made it up as an excuse to leave."

"Speaking of leaving," said Chuck, getting up from his chair. "That's our cue, Patty. It was neat hearing about the ghost, but we've got to go."

"Thanks for the cookies and the root beer," said Patty. "We've had a wonderful time and we hope that old ghost doesn't show up to frighten you."

## ᭡ 8 ᭢

# The Secret Closet

MONDAY IT RAINED. Mr. Hubbard left the house early. He had bought a small secondhand car to drive himself to and from the office.

"I suppose we need rain," said Abby, "but I just wish it would rain at night instead of in the daytime. We'd planned to meet Chuck and Patty on the beach this afternoon."

"Ask them to come here instead," Mrs. Hubbard suggested. "You can set up the Ping-pong table in the ballroom and have fun there."

"I'll call Chuck and you call Patty," said Kit.

"Tell them to come after lunch," said their mother. "Essie is cleaning downstairs this morning. Keep out of her way." She was slipping her arms into her yellow raincoat as she spoke. "I have a lot of errands to do and will market on my way home. I won't be too long."

It was no hardship to keep out of Essie's way. John's wife might be "handy" with a broom as he had said, but her personality was not appealing. She was squat of figure and unsmiling of face. Her pale eyes were red-rimmed, as though she had an allergy, or did some secret crying (Abby wondered which), and her limp putty-colored hair escaped from its bun in wisps around her face. She was partial to faded pink house dresses and white ankle socks above strapped canvas sandals. Abby thought her shapeless bare legs looked like giant white slugs. They said good morning to her as they passed her in the hall, glad to keep out of her way.

After they had phoned and issued the invitation Abby decided it was a good morning to sew. She would start work on the curtains for her room. She had bought the flower-sprinkled sheet last Saturday and had already cut the material.

While Abby opened the sewing machine in the upstairs sitting room, Kit stared moodily out of the window. The sky was sullen and swollen, with no hint of a break in the clouds. Rain fell steadily and determinedly as though it intended to continue all day. The sea was gray, its surface puckered with rain drops; the horizon was blotted out.

The only sound in the room was the hum of the sewing machine as it whirred over the pins marking the hem. He wished Abby would quit work and play chess with him. He got out the chess set and arranged the chessmen hopefully. The sewing machine stopped. Abby began removing pins from the finished hem.

"Come on and have a game of chess," he urged.

"Oh, Kit, I want to finish these and get them up before Patty and Chuck arrive. Can't you watch television or read or something?"

"TV's no good with the sewing machine going. I can't hear a thing."

He flopped into a chair by the fireplace and scratched the new mosquito bite on his calf. Girls were the lucky ones! If they had to stay indoors, they could always find things to do. They could sew or make fudge or read. But he'd read all his books and they hadn't had time to join the library yet so he could get new ones. He didn't feel like working on his stamp collection.

He stared at the fireplace. The back of it had been lined with bricks since the old days to make it look smaller. The secret closet was behind it. Aunt Ann had shown it to them last week after Chuck and Patty had gone home. You got in it by pushing on a wallpaper panel in the back of a small clothes closet off the hall to Mother's bedroom. No one would ever suspect anything was behind the panel, but when it swiveled around, there was a large dark space next to the fireplace chimney, almost like a little room.

Aunt Ann had said that Indians were unfamiliar with houses. After all they lived in tepees or lodges made of animal skins, so—even if they searched the house—they would not know enough to hunt for another closet behind the first one. She said the Indians around here had been friendly for the most part but sometimes they had taken children away to live with them. That was why, whenever Indians approached the house, the children were shooed upstairs into the hidden closet.

Without the slightest difficulty Kit transported himself to that long-ago time. From the kitchen window he'd seen two Indians flitting as silently as shadows from tree to tree. No doubt they had gotten a whiff of venison cooking and the corn pone that Ma was baking. They always expected to be fed when they came calling. He didn't need to wait for Ma to motion him toward the stairs. He was up them like a shot, as silent as the Indians. He knew where to go.

Abby, absorbed in her work, did not see Kit slip out of the room.

He let himself into the closet, closing the door quietly after him. With a press of his hand the panel swiveled around and he was in the larger secret space. It was dark and musty and he wished he had remembered to bring his flashlight. But there was not time. *Whoa! wait a minute. Something wrong there! Flashlights had not been invented yet. He would have to wish for a candle instead.* The important thing was to remain still so the Indians would not hear him.

He sank down carefully on the floor and leaned against the stone of the chimney. He could almost see his mother downstairs, trying not to show any fear, wishing she could hold her nose against the Indian smell, serving them great helpings of venison stew and wishing they would eat fast and get out of there. He hoped he wouldn't sneeze. The closet was dusty and he had a tickle in his nose. He pressed his upper lip hard.

Gradually he became aware of sounds below, voices talking. Perhaps the floorboards did not fit close against the chimney and let sounds penetrate.

All at once he came back to the present. That was Essie's voice he was hearing! Not his mother's or any Indian's. Essie was talking with someone. It must be John, though the words were not clear. Then they moved closer below him for he heard John asking, "Where are those kids?" and Essie answering, "Upstairs. The girl's sewing. I don't know what the lad's up to, but he's with her."

John's voice faded as he made some reply and Kit missed the next words. Then he heard Essie say in a despairing tone, "I wish you wouldn't, even if we do need money. We've got such a nice place here and you want to risk everything."

"Well, we're in it now. We can't get out." John's tone was grim. "Don't nag at me all the time. You know I'll be careful."

The voices ceased. He heard the side door slam and guessed that John had left. After a few minutes of silence, punctuated with a gulping sob, the sound of the vacuum began. Essie had resumed her cleaning.

Kit rose softly to his feet and slipped from his hiding place. He went silent-footed back to the sitting room. Abby looked up in surprise as he appeared.

"Abby," he whispered, "something queer is going on here."

He told her all he had overheard. Try as they would they could make no sense out of it. It seemed to them that John must be involved in something that Essie did not like and that he did not want the Hubbards to know about. They wondered what it could be.

There was no opportunity to tell Mrs. Hubbard about it during lunch because Essie was within earshot. Then the arrival of Chuck and Patty drove all thought of it from their minds.

Chuck's mother had driven them over and came in to call on Mrs. Hubbard. The two ladies took to each other at once. Mrs. Burgess was tall and slender with a wide smile

and taffy-colored hair. The youngsters left their mothers
in animated conversation and proceeded upstairs. Patty
and Chuck looked about them in frank curiosity on the
way.

"I never thought we'd get to see the inside of this wonderful old house," said Patty. "Especially after your Aunt
Ann moved out and it was closed for so long. This is your
room, Abby? I adore it! Your new curtains look neat!"

"I'm glad you like them. I worked like a dog to get them
done this morning so they'd be hung before you came. We
go through this door here to get to the ballroom."

"Am I impressed!" said Chuck. "To think we should
know anyone who has a ballroom!" He took several sliding
steps on the floor and then began to twist and whirl in the
latest dance step.

The ballroom was so interesting to the visitors the Ping-
pong table was forgotten. Patty and Chuck were full of
questions. Abby explained about the small "retiring" room
to the left of the entrance. "That's where the chaperones
used to sit to watch the dancers through that window,
and where people left their cloaks."

Chuck discovered the staircase. "Where does this go?"
he asked, taking a step down it.

"It's the way they brought refreshments up from the
kitchen," said Kit. "You ought to see how they cooked in
those days."

One by one they filed down the narrow dark stairs into
the enormous room below. Only it was different now.
As soon as Kit opened some shutters to let in light,
they noticed near the outside door a shrouded shape.
Abby went over to it and tweaked the covering off. She
was surprised to see a small, graceful writing desk.

"Well I'll be!" she said. "I don't remember this being here when Aunt Ann showed us around the house."

"I don't either," said Kit. "But maybe we just didn't notice it, there was so much else to see. It's probably something Aunt Ann hasn't moved out yet."

Abby put the covering back on the desk while Chuck and Patty looked around the old kitchen and Kit told them its history. He pulled the shutters across the windows again before he followed the others upstairs. He didn't quite know why he bothered, except that the shutters had been closed when Aunt Ann first showed them the room and he supposed they should be left that way.

Abby forgot about the desk during the furious game of Ping-pong they played. It was not until later, before she fell asleep that night, that she thought about it again. Odd, she thought, that Aunt Ann would want another desk. She had told Mother that she already had a small antique desk in her apartment. But maybe Abby had misunderstood. Maybe this was the desk Aunt Ann meant, only she had not moved it out yet.

# ❧ 9 ❧

# *The Disappearing Desk*

ABBY FELL ASLEEP easily and sweetly, dismissing Aunt Ann's desk from her mind. The rain was still falling with a soothing murmurous sound. But during the night, some time, a brisk wind began to blow, tossing the treetops and rattling the windows.

Abby awoke from deep sleep with her heart pounding. What was that sound? It came again, a creaking noise, then a thud followed by a high-pitched wail. Goose pimples popped on Abby's flesh. She was rigid with fright, cold all over. She wanted to put on her light but dared not reach out to click it on. She huddled under the covers shivering.

Had Kit heard it, too? His room was next to hers. Mother and Dad, across the hall in the ell, were too far away to hear if she could find voice to call. The wail came again,

shrill and eerie, followed by the banging noise. Was someone trying to get in? All at once, with a dreadful certainty, Abby knew that it must be the ghost. Robert, the pirate, was trying to come home.

A glow of light appeared under her door. As the door opened silently Abby found her voice and shrieked.

"Abby, Abby, it's only Mother. I didn't mean to frighten you, darling. The wind woke me up and I came to check your windows."

Abby gave a shuddering sob of relief. "Oh, Mommy, I thought you were the ghost. I heard him trying to get in."

Mrs. Hubbard switched on a light and, after making sure the rain was not blowing in, stepped over to the bed and put her arms around Abby.

"You must have been dreaming, dear."

"But I wasn't! I heard him. Listen!"

"That's just the wind. Sounds as though a door were banging. I guess I may have left the kitchen window part way open at the top and the wind sucks a door down there open and shut. I ought to go and close it."

Abby clutched her mother. "Don't go away! There it is again! That wailing sound. Don't you hear it?"

Mrs. Hubbard listened intently and Abby took courage from her mother's apparent lack of fear. "It's not a ghost. I know that for sure. There's probably some perfectly natural explanation for it, but I don't know what it is yet. We'll try to find out in the morning."

"I'm so wide awake now I don't think I'll ever get back to sleep. Stay here with me a while, Mommy."

"All right. I'll snuggle up with you for a bit after I see if Kit's windows are okay."

She was back in seconds and slid into bed beside Abby.

"I had to mop his window sills," she said, "but otherwise all is serene. It would take a lot more noise than you heard to wake Kit."

The wind was diminishing. The wailing and the thuds and bangings came infrequently. Mother was probably right, Abby thought. The wind has been causing it all. She recalled what Aunt Ann had said—that it wasn't hard to believe in ghosts in an old house on a windy night. Then she remembered she had not told Mother about the conversation Kit had overheard between Essie and John. There had been so much else to talk about at dinner she had completely forgotten. Now she poured it all out.

Mrs. Hubbard made no comment until she had finished. "How did Kit happen to be in the secret closet?" she asked.

"He got bored sitting around waiting for me to play chess with him. You know how he likes to pretend. He was playing that he was back in the olden days and was hiding from Indians."

"Are you sure he didn't make up the rest of it? I can't believe that John isn't trustworthy. He's worked for Aunt Ann a long time and she seems to have complete faith in him."

"That's so," said Abby slowly. "But I don't believe Kit could have made this up, or would have. Not about Essie saying 'We've got such a nice place here and you want to risk everything.' Or about John telling her not to nag him all the time. Oh, and there's another thing. When Chuck and Patty were here, we went down the stairs from the ballroom because they wanted to see the old kitchen and there was something wrapped up in a cloth over by the door that I'm sure wasn't there when Aunt Ann showed us around."

"Did you look to see what it was?"

"Yes, I lifted the cloth and there was a desk. A little one, but lovely."

"That seems strange."

"I thought so, too. Kit said it probably belonged to Aunt Ann, but she already has a desk from here. Remember? She told us when you were asking why she didn't want to keep that old secretary desk downstairs for herself?"

"I remember very well." Mrs. Hubbard sounded troubled.

They were silent for a while. Abby began to feel sleepy. Her mother yawned and sat up in bed. "It's high time we put all of this nonsense out of our heads and get back to sleep," she said. She leaned down and kissed Abby good night. Abby gave a contented sigh and was asleep before her mother reached the door.

Next day dawned fresh and blue and dew-spangled and sparkly. The sea glittered beyond the windows and the sky was dazzlingly bright. Abby awoke with a bounce and paddled into Kit's room.

"Time to get up, sleepy head."

Kit grunted and rolled over, burying his face in the pillow.

Abby tickled him until he squirmed and called for mercy. "It's gorgeous out! We can swim today. The rain is over! Get up, you sluggard."

That fetched him. He rubbed the sleep from his eyes and sat up, tousle-headed.

"You slept through all the excitement last night," Abby told him.

"Excitement! What?"

"The ghost. I was sure I heard him trying to get into the house and I was scared half silly. Then Mother came to see about my windows and she practically convinced me that it was the wind that made the noises I'd been hearing. And then she stayed awhile to calm me down and I remembered to tell her about John and Essie—what you heard them say."

"Wow!" said Kit. "What did she think?"

"That you'd made it up."

"But I didn't! You know I didn't. I couldn't have made up anything like that."

"That's what I told her."

"Gee, thanks!"

"But I'm not sure she believed me. She said Aunt Ann had complete faith in John. Therefore Mommy can't believe he would do anything wrong."

"Essie sure sounded scared he was."

"Hey!" said Abby. "Maybe that accounts for her eyes. Maybe she's worried all the time and does a lot of crying. Maybe she doesn't mean to be so—so unfriendly, but she has so much else on her mind she doesn't want to be bothered with us."

"We'd better keep an eye on them both," said Kit. "But we mustn't let them know."

The breakfast bell sounded from below.

"What we'd better do now is stop yakking and get dressed," said Abby. "After breakfast I want Mother to go to the old kitchen with us and look at that desk."

Breakfast over and the dishes in the dishwasher, Mrs. Hubbard willingly accompanied the two children through the living room to the unused kitchen.

"It's right over there in the corner by the door," Abby

told her. Then she gave a start of astonishment. "Why, it's gone!" she said. "It's gone!" There was no sign of a shrouded shape where it had been the day before.

"Are you sure it ever was there?" asked Mrs. Hubbard. "I mean you didn't dream it, perhaps, or just imagine it?"

"We both saw it with our own eyes!" Kit was indignant that she should doubt them.

"Then it's certainly peculiar—here yesterday and gone today. Perhaps we should ask John if he knows anything about it."

"Please don't," said Abby. "I don't think we should let him know we've seen the desk. You won't believe, Mother, that John is up to something, and of course we aren't *sure* he is, either, but if he should be, this would be one certain way of tipping him off that we're suspicious of him. And please don't say anything to Aunt Ann."

Mrs. Hubbard nodded. "No, I wouldn't want to alarm her. We'll have to tell Dad tonight, though, and ask him what to do."

But Mr. Hubbard did not come home that night. He called from the office to say he was being sent to Chicago on an urgent matter and would Mother please pack his bag and meet him at the airport with it. He didn't have time to come home to pick it up himself.

## ❧ 10 ❧

# Shadowing John

FOR THE TWO DAYS Mr. Hubbard was away Kit and Abby dogged John about the place until he accused them of being his shadows. They pretended to think this a great joke, for they did not want him to guess that they were really shadowing him, like detectives.

One afternoon they watched him polish Aunt Ann's car in the old barn which now served as a garage. Their own station wagon also lived there, and there was room, too, for John's pick-up truck in which he took Essie to the movies on Saturday nights.

"Haven't you anything better to do?" John asked them. "Seems to me you should find something more interesting than watching me put a shine on your aunt's car."

"Oh, we like it here in the barn," said Kit. "Why do you have a truck instead of a regular car?"

"You and your questions! It's a handy kind of car to have." John wiped perspiration from his face with a grimy hand, and leaned against the hood of Aunt Ann's sedan. "I can cart trash in it to the dump and load it up with groceries, and now and then get a bit of hauling to do for someone that needs it. There's only Essie and me to be riding in it so the one front seat is more than enough for us."

This seemed reasonable to Abby. John was so friendly and nice to them she began to question the suspicions she and Kit had of him.

She glanced about the dimness of the old barn, empty now of hay and oats but still giving out a faint aroma of horse. There were rakes and hoes and shovels and other garden tools neatly hanging in brackets against one wall. Flower pots were stacked in a corner and there were bushel baskets, a watering can, and old burlap bags and trowels and a cultivator as well as a lawnmower and pruning sheers. Everyday useful objects—so ordinary and commonplace they seemed to rebuke her for wild imaginings.

"I wish there were some hay in this barn," said Kit. "I've never had a chance to play in a haymow."

"Kids nowadays miss out on a lot of fun," said John. "To be sure you have advantages I didn't have as a boy, but I wouldn't want to change places with you, that I wouldn't. To grow up with horses and haymows was a good thing, I'm thinking. And using your legs! You kids today hardly know you have legs, you get carted from place to place in automobiles. But when I was your age, we walked miles—miles to school and home again for lunch, and miles back in the afternoon. And in our spare time we had chores to do."

"Oh, we have chores, too," said Kit defensively. "Abby and I have to make our beds, and we take turns setting and clearing the table, and I have to shine my own shoes. Oh, I know it doesn't seem much compared to the olden days, but we do use our legs! In school we have sports and gym and games." He was growing red in the face.

John cocked his head and gave Kit a quizzical look. "I'm not saying you're soft, mind you. I'm just saying that things are easy for you, and that's the truth."

"I guess it is, John," said Abby. "Every now and then I kind of realize how lucky we are, compared to lots of people. Especially since Uncle Jonathan left us this house. It's sort of like a dream we haven't waked up from. I can't help worrying sometimes that we may come to and find it's not true at all. John, there's something I want to ask you. Did you ever see the ghost?"

"You mean the ghost of that pirate? Miss Pingree told me about him, but I can't say as how I've ever laid eyes on him. Thought I did once—on a windy night when there was fog. Thought I saw a feller walking through the mist. He sort of limped when he walked, but when I looked close, he was gone."

"Gee!" said Kit. "Abby thought she heard him the other night when the wind blew so hard. She was scared."

"I sure was!" said Abby.

"What did you hear?" John's tone was sharp. He turned his back on them to give a final rub to the fenders of the car. Then he asked casually, "What sort of sounds would a ghost be making?"

"Bangings and bumps and a wailing sound. I thought he was trying to get in. But Mother discovered next morning that she'd left a couple of windows cracked at the top and she thinks that made enough of a draft to suck a door open and shut downstairs. The ghost could have made the wailing sound, though."

John put down his polishing cloth and turned and looked at her. "You should have been asleep and not listening to noises in the night." The sharpness had gone from his voice. "Don't be going and taking fright at a ghost that means no harm."

"I guess he doesn't mean harm," said Abby slowly. "From what Aunt Ann told us about him, he just wants to come home."

John went over to the tap and washed his hands. "Your Aunt Ann will be wondering what's keeping me," he said. "I'm driving her some place this afternoon and it's time I was off." He took down his coat from a hook on the wall and put it on, then stepped into the car. "So long. Don't get into mischief. I'll be seeing you," he called. He backed the car out of the barn and waved to them as he turned into the driveway.

Abby and Kit walked slowly back to the house. "Did you get what he said about his truck?" asked Kit. "That he used it for hauling 'for someone who needs it'?"

Abby stopped short. "I heard him but I didn't take in until this minute what that might mean! He could have taken the desk away in that truck!"

"Yes, and no one could see him do it at night. Our windows don't look out on that side of the house because the ballroom is between our rooms and that side."

"But it could have been him I *heard!* The wind might

have banged the door when the desk was taken out. Did you notice how quick he was to ask me what I did hear?"

"Yes. And another thing. He's been caretaker here all the time the house was empty. So he must have had keys to all the doors. He could have had a duplicate key made to the old kitchen door before he turned the keys over to us."

"That's right." Abby pushed open the screen door and held it for Kit. They continued on upstairs, following a plan they had already put into operation—to check the old kitchen each afternoon as soon as John left with the car. That way they would know if any other strange objects were there.

So now they entered the ballroom, went softly down the narrow stairs and slipped open the wooden shutter of the nearest window. The room was empty, just as it had been the day before. Kit slid the shutter across the window again and they went back upstairs. "I hope we don't find anything else," he said. "I'm beginning to like John."

But the next afternoon, when they looked, they found a tall sheeted shape near the door. Abby undid enough of the covering to reveal a beautiful slender antique corner cupboard. She and Kit stared at each other in dismay. This clinched it. If it had only been the desk, they might have given John the benefit of the doubt. But not now.

Dad would know what to do. He was coming home tonight. In the meantime, they would find Mother and bring her to see it. She would have to believe them now.

# ༼ 11 ༽

# The Ghost Walks

MRS. HUBBARD could not help being convinced when she saw the corner cupboard. Moreover, she had managed to find out from Aunt Ann, by a seemingly aimless question, that her own desk had been moved to her apartment along with her other possessions more than a year ago. So the desk Abby and Kit had seen in the old kitchen could not have belonged to her.

Mr. Hubbard arrived in time for dinner, driving himself from the airport in his little car which had been parked there during his absence. He hugged them each in turn and told them about his time in Chicago. "It was just some engineering puzzle I had to untangle for one of our clients," he said. "But golly, was it hot there! It makes me appreciate this house more than ever to have been away from it for a few days, to say nothing of my family!"

As soon as dinner was over and the dishes were humming away in the dishwasher, Abby and her mother joined Mr. Hubbard and Kit in the library. He wondered why they did not sit out on the lawn, but Kit told him they had something important to discuss with him and they didn't want to chance being overheard.

He listened with complete attention while they told him what had been happening during his absence. And at first he found it hard to believe. It was so incredible. But as Abby and Kit filled in the details, and Mrs. Hubbard confirmed their latest discovery of the corner cupboard, he had to believe them.

"I suppose it must still be there," he said. "You say that John waits until late at night to remove the furniture. So it should be safe for me to have a look right now. It's still light outside, but I'll take a flashlight so I won't have to open the shutters in case John should be out in the yard where he might see. You wait here. I'll be back in a jiffy."

His usually pleasant face was stern when he returned. "I saw it," he said, "and I don't like it. I don't like it at all. Not the cupboard; it's a beauty, but I don't like what it must mean."

"What are we going to do?" Mrs. Hubbard asked, worriedly.

"I've been considering calling John in and asking for an explanation. But I realize that would only warn him. He can't be in this alone. He'd need someone to help him load a piece like that on his truck.

"Also, it's hard to think of John being a thief. Yet this house and that old unused kitchen provide a perfect setup to hide stolen goods. This house is so secluded, alone as it is at the end of a road, and it has been empty for more than a year with John as caretaker. Even now, with us living here, that unused room with its outside door is isolated from the rest of the house, particularly at night when we are in bed. So it would not seem to him much of a risk to continue as before, using the old kitchen as a temporary hiding place for stolen furniture."

"Maybe John is being used by the thieves and does not realize it," Mrs. Hubbard said hopefully, running a hand through her hair until her curls stood on end.

"He'd have to be awfully gullible not to suspect there was something shady about it." Mr. Hubbard looked at Abby and Kit who were fascinated by this conversation. "You haven't said anything about this to Chuck and Pat, have you?"

"No," said Abby. "Chuck's gone off on a trip with his family and Patty hasn't been around. She's had a sore throat."

"Anyhow, we wouldn't," said Kit. "We wouldn't want to spill anything unless we were sure."

"Who do you s'pose the furniture is stolen from?" Abby wondered aloud.

"*Whom*, not *who*," corrected her mother automatically.

"Aha! Abby! That's the important question. You've put your finger right on it," said Mr. Hubbard.

"And I think I have the answer!" cried Mrs. Hubbard, her eyes brilliant. "It's just come to me. I read it in the paper but it slipped my mind until this instant! It was a small news item on an inside page. About a burglary in a country house somewhere. The only thing taken was a valuable piece of antique furniture! The story said that this was another unsolved case of selective stealing that had been baffling the State Police. Apparently there have been a good many country houses broken into when the owners have been away—and in each instance all that was taken was rare old furniture!"

"Wow!" said Kit, while Mr. Hubbard gave a long whistle.

"Nat, I believe you've hit it! It fits. Now we must think what's best to do."

"Aren't you going to call the police?" asked Abby.

"We'll certainly have to report it to them," said Mr. Hubbard. "But I am beginning to think it would be better if I do it in person tomorrow. There's too much to tell over the phone. This must be some sort of a racket that will have to be investigated quietly if the police are to get to the brains behind it. I think it will be best for us to move slowly. We don't want John to suspect we are on to him. Also we don't know how much the police may already know. It's certain they haven't been idle and what we have to tell them may be just the bit of information they need to fit into the puzzle."

Kit looked his disappointment. He wanted something to happen tonight.

"Be patient, son," said his father, guessing his thoughts. "Detectives have to be, sifting snips and pieces of information and fitting them together. If we don't raise the alarm tonight, the racket—whatever it is —will continue as usual and the police will have a chance to round up the whole gang. Now, let's try to put it out of our minds. Has anybody seen my evening paper? Ah, here it is." He handed the first section to Mrs. Hubbard. "Looks as if we are in for some bad weather. There's a hurricane coming up the coast. Turn on the radio, Abby. It's time for the eight o'clock news."

"I thought that hurricane was going out to sea," said Mrs. Hubbard. "The paper did not come today, and I've been just too busy to listen to the radio. Is it really coming this way?"

"You'll hear in a minute," said Mr. Hubbard.

Kit strolled over to the window, his mind busy with an idea that had just come to him. The sea shone silvery and pewter-toned in the dusk under a sky swollen and heavy with clouds. If a hurricane really came, there ought to be some big waves out there, he thought. He only half-heard the announcer's voice relating news of the world and of Washington and the local scene. He hoped Abby would agree to what he was going to suggest.

Then the word "hurricane" brought him back to the present. "We bring you the latest word of Hurricane Doris," the announcer was saying. "Hope of her turning out to sea has vanished. Storm warnings are out from Cape Hatteras to Provincetown. All small craft please heed. Winds of gale force are creating mountainous waves and tides. Inhabitants of low-lying areas in the Carolinas, Virginia, Maryland and New Jersey are advised to seek higher ground. This lady packs a wallop! At the rate she is moving the storm ought to reach the New England coast late tomorrow. Stay tuned to this station. Further bulletins will be brought to you throughout the night."

"Whee!" said Abby. "I'm glad you got home before it happened, Daddy. And I'm glad we are already on high ground."

Kit caught her eye and jerked his head toward the door, signaling her to follow him. Their parents were so intent on discussing the hurricane and the precautions they should take, they did not notice the children leave the room.

Abby followed Kit upstairs to her bedroom, puzzled and curious. Kit closed the door after her and then turned, his face alive with excitement. "Abby, we're going to keep watch! He's sure to move that cupboard tonight for he wouldn't dare risk having it here any longer, especially now there's a hurricane coming!"

"But how? We don't want him to catch us."

"I've got it all thought out. We'll pretend to Mother and Dad that we're tired and are going to bed early. We'll fix pillows in our beds so it will look as though we are there asleep if either of them should peek in on us. And we'll sneak into the ballroom and watch from the window above the outside door. Whoever helps John will have to get himself over here by car. When they load the corner cupboard and take it away in the truck, I mean to go outside with my flashlight and get the license number of the other guy's car."

Abby sat on her bed and bounced up and down. "Kit, that's a knockout plan!" she said. "Oh, I hope we can stay awake! It would be too awful if we went in there and then fell asleep on the windowseat while everything was happening."

"I'll pinch you and you pinch me," said Kit with a grin.

Mr. and Mrs. Hubbard were a bit surprised when Abby and Kit came in to say an early good night. Kit yawned so deeply and Abby was so convincing about wanting to turn in with a new book she was reading that they accepted this unusual behavior at face value.

Soon after ten o'clock the two crept into the dark silent ballroom leaving lifelike pillow "sleepers" under the covers of their beds. Both wore blue jeans, dark sweaters, and sneakers, so they could move silently and invisibly in the dark. Kit shaded his flashlight with the palm of his hand,

producing only a glimmer of light on the floor to guide
them to the seat above the outside door. They slid the
window open an inch from the bottom and settled themselves to wait. The night had turned very dark, the wind
was rising. They could see trails of fog blowing past the
trees and collecting in pools on the ground.

For a long time they sat there, not speaking. Now and

then Kit's head would nod and Abby would touch him awake. When she nodded, he did the same for her.

Finally a faint glow of headlights showed through the mist and they heard the sound of a car approaching. At once they were wide-awake, hearts beating fast. This must be John's partner in crime. The car slowed to a stop at the approach to their driveway. The lights went out.

Listening intently they heard another car—John's truck—moving ever so cautiously along the driveway to the side entrance near the unused kitchen. The truck stopped and they saw John get out. A dark figure emerged from the fog and joined John's shadowy shape near the house. Below them they could hear the key turn in the lock and the door creak open. The figures disappeared within.

Abby's held breath came out in a tremulous sigh and Kit squeezed her hand hard. In a moment the men came out carrying the tall wrapped cupboard and Abby and Kit heard them grunt as they lifted it onto the rear of John's pickup truck. Both men got into the truck and it moved slowly down the drive and into the road.

Kit scrambled to his feet. He didn't know how long John and the other would be gone, but he didn't want to waste any time. They needn't worry about noise now. They raced across the ballroom to the stairway, Kit's flashlight showing them the way.

"You wait here," Kit told Abby when they reached the outside door. "I'll be as quick as I can." He turned the doorknob and let himself out.

Abby waited tense and shivering by the half-open door. She could see Kit's flashlight flickering along the ground. Then the mist swallowed him.

The minutes seemed endless. The fog swirled and eddied and blew in damp gusts against her face.

What was that? She heard a sound that sent chills chasing down her spine—a high-pitched wail, almost as much a screech as a wail. She recognized it at once. She had heard it before on a night of wind and rain. It was the ghost. He must be out there somewhere wanting to get in.

Abby could not have moved if she had tried. She was frozen to the spot. Before her frightened eyes the mist parted and she saw an indistinct tall figure in a long cape. He seemed to walk with a limp. Fog swirled around his head, hiding his face. Then as quickly as he had appeared he was gone. Only the cold clammy mist was there——

——and the sound of running feet. Kit nearly knocked her over in his haste to get inside and close the door. "I've got it, I've got it," he cried. "I wrote it down on a piece of paper so I couldn't forget. It's 30215! Why, Abby, what's the matter? You're shivering and shaking!"

"I'm all right," babbled Abby, "but the ghost! I saw the ghost out there in the fog!"

"Holy Henry!" said Kit.

Without regard for noise, they both raced for the stairs.

## ❧ 12 ❧

# Hurricane Doris

THEY WOKE THEIR PARENTS at once. Mr. Hubbard switched on the lamp and sat up in bed. "What in the world are you two doing here at this hour?" he asked, glancing at the electric clock on the bedside table. "It's past midnight!"

"What's the matter?" asked Mrs. Hubbard in a sleepy voice.

"We did it! We got his license number!" exclaimed Kit. "Now you can find out who he is!"

"Who *who* is? What do you mean—got his license number? How?"

"John's helper. The guy who came to help him move the cupboard," Kit told him, stumbling over the words in his haste to explain all that had happened.

After a moment of stunned silence Mr. Hubbard said,

"Very enterprising of you, Kit. I don't know why I didn't think of doing that myself."

"I know it's not so important," said Abby, "but I saw the ghost."

"Oh, you didn't!" said her mother. "You couldn't have."

"But I did!"

They listened to her account with disbelief on their faces. Then Mr. Hubbard said, "You were nervous and excited waiting for Kit. Your imagination played you a trick, Pumpkin. It was probably just a bush you saw that looked like a ghost in the fog."

"That must have been it," said Mother, "and now you must get back to bed. I'll come and tuck you in."

"A good night's work, son," said Mr. Hubbard. "First thing in the morning I'll go to the State Police."

The next day was overcast with a leaden sky. The wind had quieted, but the air was heavy and oppressive. Dad had already left the house when the children came down.

Abby felt cross and out of sorts from lack of sleep and from apprehension, both because of the coming hurricane and because she didn't know what was going to happen next. In broad daylight it was hard for her to believe that she had really seen the ghost, yet she was indignant that the family doubted her. She hoped she would not have to meet John face to face or talk with him. She would be afraid to look him in the eye, afraid he would guess from her expression that she and Kit had spied on him, that they knew about what had been going on last night. Even now Dad might be talking with the police officers. They might be getting ready this very moment to close in on him. It gave her an uneasy feeling.

Mrs. Hubbard hustled Kit and Abby through breakfast and bedmaking and asked them to go with her to the market. "We need to buy candles and some Sterno to cook over in case the power fails, and I want to lay in extra supplies of food, canned goods and such. There are some old oil lamps in the kitchen closet and we'll need kerosene for them," she said, busy with her list at the kitchen table.

"Get some hamburger and some hot dogs," said Kit. "We can cook in the fireplace." He was elated at the prospect and so full of suppressed energy he couldn't keep his feet or hands still.

"You act as though a hurricane were going to be fun!" said his mother, grinning up at him. "Put on your raincoats and let's go. It looks as though it would pour any minute."

It was blowing again when they went outside. The wind seemed to be coming from all directions at once. They hung on to their rain hats and fought the wind to the car. The big supermarket in Thetford was crowded with people on the same errands, to stock up with necessities before the storm struck. Abby and Kit darted here and there to select from the shelves the items Mrs. Hubbard told them to get while she chose the meats at the meat counter. Finally with loaded cart they waited their turn at the cashier's turnstile and then carried the heavy bags to their car.

Large drops of rain fell as they put the last bag in the rear of the station wagon. Mrs. Hubbard started the motor and turned on the radio. Static sounded through music but then they heard a voice saying clearly, "Hurricane Doris is striking the Jersey shore a serious blow. High tides have flooded streets in Atlantic City. Winds of one hundred miles an hour are ripping off roofs, flailing trees, toppling signs, smashing plate glass windows in hotels and stores. Long Island and the New England coast may expect the full brunt of the storm by late afternoon. All small craft are advised to take immediate shelter."

By the time they reached home the rain was coming down hard and the wind was lashing it in sheets against the windshield so the wipers could not keep up with it. Mrs. Hubbard drove around to the rear of the house and stopped the car opposite the kitchen door. They had to run for it, each carrying a bag of groceries, the wind buffeting them and the rain whipping into their faces and cascading off the brims of their rain hats. Laughing and exhilarated they dumped their bags on the kitchen counter while water dripped off their slickers onto the floor.

"Phew-ee," said Mrs. Hubbard. "It's really begun! Run upstairs and fill the bathtubs with water while I fill some bottles and put them in the icebox. If the current goes off our pump will stop working and we won't have any water."

"Water, water, everywhere and not a drop to drink," chanted Abby as she and Kit shed their raincoats and hastened to do their mother's bidding.

From then on the storm grew steadily worse. Gusts of wind shook the house, sent rain smashing against the windows, bent the treetops so they writhed and twisted, tore clumps of leaves from the boughs. The big oak that grew outside Abby's bedroom window groaned in protest. Rain blotted out the sea but they could hear waves crashing against the bluff. The noise of the storm grew worse.

Mrs. Hubbard was fixing sandwiches for lunch when there came a hammering on the kitchen door. It was John, dripping water, come to ask if they were all right. Abby was in the library so she did not have to face him and

Mrs. Hubbard reported that he seemed cheerful in spite of the hurricane and wanted to be helpful if needed. He borrowed her car keys and put the car away in the barn. That made Abby feel worse about him.

Kit beat Abby to the phone when it rang. When he picked up the receiver no one was on. The phone had gone dead.

"I wish Daddy were home," said Mrs. Hubbard worriedly. "If he doesn't come soon, he may not be able to get here."

"Why not?" asked Abby.

"I'm afraid trees may blow down across the road."

But at two o'clock he arrived soaking wet from the dash from his car to the house. "The office closed early on account of the storm," he told them. "A good thing, too, or I never would have made it. A tree crashed behind me down the road. Just missed me, and now no one can get through until it's cleared away."

"Wow!" said Kit. "Ma was worried and she had reason to be!"

*No one can get through.* The words echoed in Abby's mind. That meant the police could not come to get John today. She didn't know whether to be sorry or glad. "Tell us what the police said about John," she begged.

"Let me get into some dry clothes first. Then I'll have quite a tale to tell you." He stepped over to the wall and flicked the light switch. Nothing happened. "I thought so," he said. "That tree took the electric wires with it. Hope you got a good supply of candles, Nat. We're going to need them."

# ∽ 13 ∽

# "A Temporary Hiding Place"

ABBY WENT UPSTAIRS to get a book from her room. Rain was leaking in around her windowpanes. She got a towel from the bathroom and mopped up the water; then after wringing the towel, she wadded it along her window sill. Water was falling in sheets outside and lashing against the house. The wind howled and raged. High above it she heard once again that weird spine-chilling sound she had heard before. It did not seem as frightening, somehow, in the daytime and surely no ghost would appear while it was still light outside.

She pressed her face against the window to try to see through the rain. Another sound made her jump—a sharp crack as a great bough from the oak tree fell to the ground with a crash. Then the wailing noise came again ending in a screech. She craned her neck to look upward in the direction of the sound and she had to laugh at herself when she saw what was causing it. It was produced by the friction of wood against wood! Another oak branch, growing at a right angle to the house, was rubbing itself against the edge of the roof each time the wind forced it there.

So that was what she had thought was the ghost trying to get in! Mother had said there would be a natural explanation and there was! She felt a little let down. She *wanted* the house to have a ghost, and she still believed she had seen him, in spite of the natural explanation about the bush that Dad had suggested. Would there be a "natural explanation" for the stolen furniture, too, she wondered? She picked up her book and hastened downstairs.

Kit had lit a fire in the library fireplace to make it seem more cozy and to be ready with good hot coals for cooking hamburgers for supper. Mrs. Hubbard touched a match to the candles on the mantel. "We might as well have some light," she said. "It's so dismal outside you'd think it was evening instead of mid-afternoon. I've made tea for Dad and myself. There's ginger ale on the ice if you want some. The ice won't last long with the current off."

Mr. Hubbard appeared in flannel slacks and a V-necked pullover. He sank into a deep chair and lighted his pipe, then gave a contented sigh. "It's a good feeling," he said as he stubbed out the match, "to be safe under your own roof with your family close by when a storm is raging outside."

"I must confess I like it, too," said Mrs. Hubbard. "Only I'm scared for any people caught outdoors or on the sea."

"Tell us what happened today," urged Kit. "What did the State Police tell you?"

Mr. Hubbard took a sip of tea from his cup and set it down again while Abby swallowed some ginger ale and waited impatiently.

"As I told you, it's quite a tale. The first officer I spoke to turned me over to a captain of detectives named Deevers. And when I told him my story, he said this was just the break they had been waiting for. It seems that there has been a rash of robberies over the past several years—and in each case the robbers have been extremely selective—taking only some rare old pieces of furniture from country houses when the owners were away, and leaving other valuables untouched. Now this is the funny thing, there is never any clue as to what happened to the furniture after it was stolen. It has never turned up for sale anywheres; it has just vanished. And because of this lack of further developments the newspapers have carried only the one initial story of each random theft.

"The State Police sensed a pattern in the thievery. They became convinced that the thefts were related, that some master plan was involved. But until today they had nothing tangible to go on. Kit, Captain Deevers asked me to congratulate you on your enterprise in getting that car license. He thinks it will help break the case."

"Is that all you know," asked Abby, disappointed. "What is going to happen to John?"

"It's not quite all I know, Pumpkin," said her father, amused. "While I was at the police office, a call was made to the Motor Vehicle Bureau headquarters and in a short while a report came back about the owner of the car. It belongs to an employee of an antique shop in Haven City. Isn't that a suggestive coincidence? But even more suggestive is the fact that the antique shop has been under suspicion for some time as being a bit shady in its business practices. The big question now is where the furniture was taken after it left here. Our old unused kitchen was obviously just a temporary hiding place. The man who owned the car—his name is Folsom, is being shadowed from now on in the hope he will lead the police to the brains behind the scheme or racket, whichever you'd call it. John won't be questioned until later. For the time being, the police do not wish him to suspect that they are on to his partner. I tried to say some good things for him, but he certainly must have known he was doing something wrong. Even though he wasn't stealing himself, he was hiding stolen goods and that's a crime."

"Oh, I hope it will turn out all right," said Mrs. Hubbard. "Ann depends on him so. It will be an awful blow to her if she finds he's mixed up with thieves."

"Just think of all the things he could have let them steal from this house," said Abby, "and he didn't! It must have been a temptation, too, with all the beautiful antiques Aunt Ann left here. But he didn't let those others take them."

"When are we going to know the rest of the story?" asked Kit.

His father stretched his legs and tapped his pipe out in the ash tray. "The police are going to have to move very cautiously. But Captain Deevers promised to keep in touch and to let me know the outcome. So we'll just have to wait and see."

They had been so intent on what Mr. Hubbard had been saying they had ceased to be aware of the storm. But now the howl of the wind and the pounding of the rain penetrated again. The windows rattled in their frames and the house groaned and creaked like a ship at sea. Kit went to the radio, but when he flicked it on, the dial failed to light up. He realized at once that with the electricity off it would not operate. "I wish we had a battery set," he said.

They cooked hamburgers in a long-handled grill over the hot coals in the fireplace and Mrs. Hubbard heated vegetable soup over a can of Sterno. With cold milk and a slice of cake for dessert, they made a good supper and all agreed that food had never tasted better.

Somewhere around eight o'clock there was a brief lull in the wind. The sudden quiet was so noticeable Kit thought the hurricane had been turned off like a tap. But in a short while the wind was howling as wildly as ever and rain fell in torrents. "That must have been the eye of the storm," Mr. Hubbard said. "At this rate the hurricane should pass over in a few hours."

To Abby the "eye of the storm" was an odd expression. She visualized a huge fierce eye peering down on them from the midst of the vortex of wind and rain.

She and Kit played checkers before the fire in which the paper plates and cups they had used for supper were burning merrily. No dishes to bother with. That was one good thing about a hurricane!

As Mr. Hubbard had predicted, the storm moved on and by ten o'clock the wind and rain had ceased. When they looked out, a full moon rode the heavens, illuminating fallen trees and downed branches. Only the sea was still restless and angry.

"We shall have to wait until tomorrow to see the full extent of the damage," said Mr. Hubbard. "The linesmen and repairmen from the light companies will be working all night, I expect, to get service established again. So we can hope to have electricity by morning."

# ❦ 14 ❧

# The Smugglers' Tunnel

THE NEXT DAY dawned serene and calm with a sky of lark-spur blue washed clean of clouds. Abby could hardly believe that there had been a hurricane. From her window she could see John already out raking up the litter the storm had left on the lawn. When she came downstairs, her mother announced with pleasure that the electricity was on and that nothing in the refrigerator had spoiled during the time the current was off.

"We are lucky to escape so lightly," said her father. "I hope that tree has been removed so I can get to the office. I'm going in, even though it is Saturday, to catch up on my work." He took a final sip of coffee.

"The radio reports lots of damage," said Mrs. Hubbard. "Beach houses demolished, roads washed out, bridges down, streets flooded, but no lives lost. And that's a miracle. The Red Cross is feeding the homeless in churches and schools turned over as temporary shelters."

"Gosh," said Kit, arriving in time to hear this recital of disaster, "I hope Chuck's and Patty's houses are still there."

"Let's go see as soon as we've had breakfast," said Abby.

The air outside was crisp and sparkling. The sea stretched limitless and blue to the horizon, unwrinkled by waves, but strangely empty. John hailed them as they crossed the lawn. "Going to look at what the sea washed up?" he asked. "Now's the time, before the tide gets any further in. You wouldn't think that there sea could have kicked up such a rumpus to look at it now!"

"You sure wouldn't, the way it was pounding and crashing against the bluff last night," said Kit.

"We want to see if our friends' houses are still there," said Abby. She hurried Kit along for she felt uncomfortable talking with John.

They saw that the picket fence had been blown down. Only the white gateposts remained tilted crazily toward the house. The path was nearly obliterated—the stone steps dislodged, some of them missing, and there were places where there just wasn't any path. They picked their way gingerly, sending pebbles and stones clattering before them.

The beach below was strewn with seaweed and shells and pieces of driftwood. A fat old herring gull waddled away at their approach and a hermit crab scuttled for shelter. Sandpipers teetered along the water's edge and gulls screamed and soared overhead, swooping down to snatch small fish from the creaming fringes of the waves as they slid up the sand.

Abby breathed deeply of the salty briny smell. She gazed anxiously up the beach toward the distant row of summer cottages. As nearly as they could make out, most of them still stood, but as they drew near they saw that the house next to Patty's had lost its roof and another house had been knocked off its foundation. Sand was piled high on verandahs, lying in drifts against front doors, spilling over porch steps.

"What a mess!" exploded Kit. "I'm glad I don't have to clean it up!"

"Those poor people! But it looks as though they all got away before it happened. I don't see a sign of life!"

Kit nodded. "Chuck said he wouldn't be here until next week. I suppose Patty and her family went home to Haven City before the hurricane got bad."

"Oh, I hope she'll call us up—that is—when the phones get fixed, and if her sore throat's better so she can talk."

They had turned and were walking slowly back the way they had come, lingering over each new discovery, fascinated by the curious treasures they found along the beach. They were unaware of time. Kit straightened up from examining the empty shell of a horseshoe crab. He was facing toward the bluff. "Holy Henry!" he exclaimed, pointing. "Will you look at that!"

Coming down the bluff path, they had had to keep their eyes so closely on their footing that they had not really seen what the pounding sea had done to the face of the bluff. Bushes and undergrowth had been torn out by the roots, and at one spot farther on, where the beach narrowed beyond the curve of the bluff, they could see that the surface had been undermined by the waves, hollowing out an overhang at the top and exposing vertically slanting ridges of protruding rock. From the lower base of one rocky ridge, a large slab of stone had broken away and had fallen on the sand. Where it had been, partly concealed by a tangle of roots and torn shrubs, was a crevice—a narrow opening showing black against the color of the bluff.

"It looks like a cave," cried Kit, running toward it with Abby at his heels. He ventured in a step or two, hunching his shoulders together to make himself small. "It seems to be deep," he called to Abby. "I can't discover any end to it."

"Do you s'pose it's a tunnel?" asked Abby.

Kit backed out and turned to face her. "Did you say tunnel?" He stared at her openmouthed, his eyes blazing. "The smugglers' tunnel! Abby, it must be! I'd forgotten all about it but this must be it!"

Abby hopped up and down. "It has to be! Run back to the house and get a flashlight. We ought to explore it right away and we won't be able to see anything without a light."

Kit turned and dashed for the path. Its steepness slowed him.

Abby sat on the warm sand, hugging her knees and gazing unseeingly out across the waters of the Sound. She was lost in the excitement of her thoughts about the tunnel. She did not observe how much nearer the foamy fingers of the waves were advancing on the sand. She was brought back to reality by Kit's voice. He was out of breath from running, but he held the flashlight in his hand. "I didn't tell Ma what we were up to, for she might not like it," he panted.

"Smart boy!" Abby jumped to her feet. "You lead the way," she said. She wouldn't have admitted it, but she did not feel too brave about stepping into that dark damp tunnel.

If they had been any taller they would have had to stoop to get inside. It was cool and dark, but the beam of their light showed the walls becoming wider ahead, amply wide and high enough for one grown person to slip through at a time. The walls dripped water and there were shells and sea snails clinging to them. For a while daylight from the opening seeped into the darkness, then the tunnel took a turn and the light behind was cut off.

At first they did not speak. Finally Kit could not suppress the triumph he felt. "Abby, you're right! This has to be it! We've found the smugglers' tunnel!" His voice sounded odd and muffled.

"If it is, it will lead to our cellar," said Abby. Then she thought of something else. "We won't be able to get in, because that entrance must have been sealed up, too, and that's why it never has been found!"

This prospect did not daunt Kit. "Let's keep on anyway. We won't know for sure unless we do."

The light of Kit's flash showed that the tunnel sloped upward. They moved ahead slowly, feeling their way. Abby wondered what kind of men had traveled this path before. Long, long ago sailors must have rowed to the beach outside from vessels anchored offshore. They had walked this same way! She could see them carrying heavy burdens on their shoulders—goods that the colonists needed but could not get except by smuggling, unless they paid excessive taxes to England. Perhaps even pirates had used this tunnel!

Kit was being extra cautious. He flashed the light overhead to make sure that the roof of the tunnel would hold.

The beams that supported it were ancient. What if the roof caved in on them? Abby for the first time began to think they had not been so smart after all not to let anyone know where they were.

She noticed that it was getting wet underfoot. She could feel water seeping up between her bare toes. In no time the damp cold had crept almost to her ankles. All at once she was struck with a terrible realization. "Kit," she gasped, grabbing him by the arm, "the tide is coming in! Don't you feel the water? It's getting deeper!"

Kit had not been thinking about tides. Now he whirled around, shining his light back the way they had come. It showed water lapping against the sides of the tunnel. Even as they watched, the wet edged further up the wall.

"We'd better get out of here! And quick!" he said.

This time Abby was in the lead as they splashed back the way they had come. But with each step they took on the downward slope, the water deepened. Before long it was up to their knees.

Abby stopped so abruptly Kit bumped into her and nearly sent her sprawling. "What's the matter? Don't stop now. We've got to hurry!"

"It's no use," said Abby despairingly. "Don't you see, if it's this deep already by the time we get to the opening the water will have closed it off! We're trapped! We can't get out!"

# ✂ 15 ✂

# *Trapped*

KIT WAS SILENT for so long Abby thought he did not comprehend. "We're trapped in here," she repeated. "Kit, don't you understand?"

Kit shivered. "I understand. Sure I do. I was just trying to think."

"What will we do?" wailed Abby. "I don't want to drown!" She jiggled up and down trying to keep warm. The realization of their plight chilled her even more than the cold water.

"It won't do any good to panic," said Kit firmly. "All we have to do is to turn around and follow the tunnel to the end. The tide won't come as high as the tunnel has to climb to reach the house, so we'll be safe. When the tide goes out, we'll go with it."

Abby tried to control the chattering of her teeth. "How long will that be?" she asked as they started splashing back up the sloping passage.

"That was what I was trying to figure. The tide takes about six hours to come in and the same time to go out."

Abby gave a groan of dismay.

"Oh, we won't have to wait that long! It must be nearly full now. Low tide was at six this morning. I know because I looked at the tide chart in my room." He flashed the light on his watch. "It's past eleven now so we won't have such a long time to wait before it turns."

Kit was so matter-of-fact Abby felt better. She told herself she must try to be as calm and brave as he was. But she had another fear she tried to suppress. Would there be enough air for them to breathe before the outgoing tide uncovered the mouth of the tunnel? If they didn't have to drown, they just might suffocate instead. The air was already close, with a musty mouldy smell. She took light quick breaths in order to use less oxygen and wondered, with sudden concern, what their mother would do when they failed to show up for lunch.

As they moved forward Kit's flashlight showed that the walls of the tunnel were less damp. The water became progressively more shallow underfoot. After a few more yards the slope of the tunnel leveled off and they realized they were beyond the reach of the tide. Ahead was a blank wall. No, it was a door! The light shown on a heavy timbered door set into what had to be the wall of their cellar. It had crossbars of rusty iron and a hole for a key, but no door handle.

Kit ran his hands over the ancient wood surface and along the edges where it fitted snugly into the door frame

in the wall. He pushed with all his might. The door refused to budge. "It must be locked," he said. "We'll just
have to sit out the tide."

"Mommy used to talk about sitting out dances, but I
never heard of anyone sitting out a tide!" said Abby.
"We'll be the first!" She felt a little lightheaded with relief, feeling certain now that they would not drown. She
pushed the other fear out of her thoughts. Surely there
would be enough air to last the hour or so they would
have to be here.

"Well, let's sit then," said Kit, proceeding to do so. His
teeth were chattering and his legs felt full of goose bumps
and waterlogged.

Abby sank down facing away from him. "Lean your
back against mine," she suggested. "That way our backs
will keep warm." Heavy darkness pressed down on them
as he switched off the light. When Abby protested he
said, "We don't want the battery to give out."

The floor of the tunnel here was dry and powdery.
Abby wiggled about trying to find a comfortable position.
Her toes touched something small and hard which moved
at her touch. She jerked her feet away. Whatever it was,
it did not feel alive.

"Stop wiggling," said Kit. "Can't you keep still?"

"My toes touched something. Lend me the flash a
minute. I want to see what it is."

She beamed the light at the object. There was an answering dimmer gleam from the tunnel's floor. She
reached out and picked up an irregularly round flat disk,
about the size of a silver dollar.

"Look what I found!" she cried. Kit swiveled toward
her and they both examined what appeared to be a silver

coin. It had an inscription on one side which they could not make out.

"It's in some foreign language," said Kit, after a minute. He read off the letters, HISPANIARUM ET IND, REX."

Abby tried to pronounce them. "REX means king in Latin. I know that much. But what does ET IND mean? HISPANIARUM." She sounded the word over and over on her tongue. "Spain! I'll bet it means Spain! There's a king's crown over a shield, like a coat of arms. Maybe it's a piece of eight!"

"Golly, I'll bet it is! But I wish it were a gold doubloon!"

Both of them had read tales of pirate treasure dredged up from sunken vessels, Spanish ships which had gone down in storms or battles with rich cargoes of jewels and gold doubloons and pieces of eight. That odd term for money had puzzled them until they had looked it up in the dictionary and learned that a "piece of eight" was a *peso*, or Spanish dollar, equal to eight coins of lesser value called "reales," hence named a "piece of eight."

"Someone must have dropped it here," said Abby, startled by this thought. It brought the early users of the tunnel closer.

"I wonder if there are any more," said Kit. He reached for the flashlight and began turning over the powdery sand on the tunnel's floor. Abby sifted sand through her fingers, without result. That was the only coin they found.

She began to feel drowsy. Kit complained of being hungry. Then his head commenced to nod, too. They both slept. Minutes passed before Abby struggled awake. This would never do! She shook herself and poked Kit. "We've been asleep," she said. "What time is it now?"

Kit found it difficult to focus on his watch. Every movement was an effort.

"Why it's quarter to one!" he said amazed. "We've been here over an hour. I don't feel right. What's the matter with me?"

"I feel queer, too," said Abby. "I think it's because of the stale old air in here." She arose stiffly and pulled him to his feet. "Let's try to get out, the tide should have turned by now."

They moved slowly and groggily back the way they had come. As they descended the air became easier to breathe. Much of the water had already drained away and fresh air filtered in through the tunnel opening.

It revived them. They splashed the last distance. As they turned the bend in the tunnel and approached its mouth the brilliance of the light outside nearly blinded them. The water was up to their knees here. They waded through the opening and then made for the beach, exultant and exhausted.

# ✂ 16 ✂

# *No Door*

As ABBY FEARED, their mother had been worried. "Where *have* you been?" she asked as they came into the kitchen. She was just finishing icing a chocolate cake. "I rang the lunch bell a long time but you never came."

When they told her she was astonished and horrified. "That was a terribly risky thing for you to do! If I had known what you were up to my hair would have stood on end. The smugglers' tunnel! Your Aunt Ann didn't believe there really was one. What will she say when she hears about this! And to think that you two found it!" Her pride in them turned to dismay. "My goodness, you're damp and dirty. Hie yourselves upstairs and get into some clean clothes quick. I'll have something for you to eat when you come down."

Lunch for Kit consisted of three hot dogs encased in rolls, a bowl of cole slaw, two glasses of milk and a slab of the freshly made chocolate cake. He felt completely restored when he was finished. Abby stowed away a considerable amount, too, though her capacity could not equal Kit's. Mrs. Hubbard sat with them at the kitchen table and continued her questions. She was especially interested and thrilled over the piece of eight. She studied it closely, then suggested Abby put it in an envelope in her desk.

"I can hardly wait to have you tell Aunt Ann about this," she said. "The phone is still out of order so we'll have to drive over to see her. She's probably anxious about us anyhow, wondering if the house was damaged and how we survived the hurricane."

"I want to go down cellar first," said Kit. "I don't see why the door we saw doesn't show from the inside."

"We'll all go," said Mrs. Hubbard.

They left the dishes on the table and went through the dining room into the old part of the house. The cellar stairs decended from the center hall by way of a door opening at the rear of the main staircase. Mrs. Hubbard switched on the cellar light and Kit went first down the narrow steps. The furnace and a fuel oil storage tank stood in one corner, the hot water heater and the electric water pump in another. To their right an open doorway led to the newer cellar under the dining room and kitchen, used for storage. Overhead were huge old beams, interlaced with water pipes and cables carrying electric wires.

The cellar walls were of masonry made of uneven rough stones set in oyster-shell mortar. The light bulb dangling from the ceiling threw distorted shadows before them as they moved toward the south wall on the seaward side of the house. Mrs. Hubbard's shadow topped Abby's and Kit's and moved up the wall above theirs as they approached. There was no sign of any door in the wall. It stretched solid and massive, in every respect like the other three walls of the cellar.

"This is darn funny-peculiar," said Kit. "The door we saw was made of heavy timbers and had crossbars of rusty looking iron. It must have opened into this cellar once. There's no place else for it to go."

"But you didn't really expect to find a door down here, did you?" his mother asked. "Aunt Ann said no door had ever been discovered."

Kit shrugged. "No, I guess I didn't," he said, "but I don't see why it isn't here." He scratched his head in bafflement. Then he noticed that Abby had started pacing off the floor from that wall to the one opposite, placing one foot ahead of the other with heel touching toe, holding her arms out from her shoulders to help keep her balance. "What, for Pete's sake, do you think you are doing?" he asked.

Abby did not answer. She just kept going until she reached the opposite wall. It did not take long for Kit to catch on. "You're measuring!" he exclaimed. "How many of your feet?"

"Forty-four. I don't know how many real feet that would be. We'll have to measure my foot then multiply it by forty-four and divide by twelve to find out. But what I want to do now is go upstairs and walk this way from end to end of the living room to see if it measures the same. If it's longer than down here, we'll know that this wall was built to conceal the tunnel door."

"Thata girl! That's using the old noggin," said Mrs. Hubbard. "Why not my feet, they're longer than yours? It wouldn't take so many of them!"

"Not on your life! I thought of it first," said Abby, making for the stairs ahead of Kit and her mother. She ran across the hall into the living room.

"A yardstick would be better than your feet," said Kit as he caught up with her, "or a tape measure."

"We've started with my feet and I mean to finish with them!" Abby was stubborn about it. She began to pace off the distance from wall to wall, side-stepping around furniture when it got in her way, counting aloud. When she came to forty-four, she was still some distance from the front of the house. The count of fifty-two brought her there.

"You see!" She turned in triumph. "This means there must be space between that wall down there and the original cellar wall with the door in it!"

Kit went to the library and came back with a ruler. "Here, measure your foot."

Abby placed the ruler on the floor and her foot along side it. "Eight inches," she said. "Where's a pencil and paper?"

Mrs. Hubbard fetched those and she and Kit worked out the problem, too. Fifty-two of Abby's feet, eight inches long, equaled four hundred and sixteen inches, divided by twelve inches (a linear foot), became thirty-four feet eight inches, the length of the living room. They checked each other's answers and found them all the same. The second translation of Abby's feet into linear measure for the cellar resulted in twenty-nine feet, four inches.

"That's a difference of five feet four inches," said Mrs. Hubbard. "Five feet four inches of space behind the cellar wall! I never would have guessed it."

"But it won't be that much," said Kit. "Don't forget we have to allow for the thickness of the wall. They built them awful thick in those days. If we allow twenty-four inches for the wall, which is only a guess, that slices down the space behind it to about three feet."

"What I wonder is why the wall was ever built in the first place," said Abby.

"I mean to find out what's behind it," said Kit. "Even if we have to tear it down."

"Your father will have something to say about that," said Mrs. Hubbard.

"You know he'll be just as curious as we are," said Abby.

Her mother laughed. "You're right. Put the arithmetic away in my desk, Abby. If we're going to see Aunt Ann this afternoon we had better get started. I'll go get the car."

# ❧ 17 ❧

# Aunt Ann's Revelation

"John was in the barn and I told him where we are going," said Mrs. Hubbard as they rolled down the driveway. "He said Aunt Ann could not get through to him by phone, but I'm to let him know if she wants him to drive her to church tomorrow."

They had no trouble reaching Aunt Ann's street in Thetford but they saw much damage from the storm on the way. There were uprooted trees, shutters torn from windows, roofs buckled in. Miss Pingree lived on the first floor in an old house which had been converted into apartments. Branches littered the lawn. The driveway to the house was blocked by the fallen trunk of a large maple.

Miss Pingree greeted them with delight. "A sight for

sore eyes, you are!" she cried. "Come in, come in. I've
been trying to get you on the phone all day but it's still
not working. I've been so concerned for your safety. I
must say, though, you all look as fit as fiddles. Tell me
about the house. It's stood against many a storm before
so I expect it held out against this one."

"It only lost a few shingles," said Mrs. Hubbard. "A big
limb was torn off that old oak in front of Abby's window,
and the fence blew down, but those are minor. We know
we are lucky."

"Find yourselves comfortable seats, Abby and Kit. The
kettle's on and I'll make us some tea. I use gas so the
current going off didn't inconvenience my cooking. I
made cookies just hoping you'd turn up." She beamed
at them, motioning Mrs. Hubbard to follow her. "You
may help me, Natalie. I'll show you where the teacups are
and you fix the tray."

She led the way out of the room, her fluffy white head
reminding Abby once again of a gone-to-seed dandelion
above the slender stem of her green dress.

The room they were in was pleasantly large but somewhat overcrowded with sofas and chairs and little tables
and corner whatnots filled with curios. Abby could see
why Aunt Ann had not needed any more furniture. Above
the mantel hung the portrait of a stern-faced old man in
a carved gilt frame, one of their Pingree ancestors. There
were other family portraits on the walls and Abby took
a good look at the delicate antique desk between two
windows. She realized at once that it was not the desk
she had found in the old kitchen.

Aunt Ann returned bearing a plate of thin crisp sugar
cookies with nuts and cherries on top. Their mother fol-

lowed with the silver tea tray which she placed on a low table near Aunt Ann's tall wing chair.

Miss Pingree seated herself and poured tea into delicate china cups. Its fragrance was delicious.

"Sugar and milk in yours, Abby? That's the way the English like it."

Kit wanted his that way, too, but their mother said she liked the Chinese way best and took hers plain.

Abby handed around the cups and passed the cookies.

"These two have only just finished lunch," said Mrs. Hubbard. "I don't know where they find room to put any more food."

"Always room in the hold," said Kit, patting his stomach.

Aunt Ann smiled. "Why so late with lunch?" she asked.

This was the opening the children had been waiting for. "Because we were too busy finding the smugglers' tunnel!" they said.

"You what?" Her amazement was delightfully satisfying. She continued to make Oh's and Ah's of astonishment at each new revelation in their story and expressed concern over the danger they had been in.

"I never would have believed it," she said, at last. "So there was truth in that old legend after all! And a false wall in the cellar that no one ever suspected."

"What's bothering us now," said Abby, "is why the second wall happened to be built. Why did someone long ago want to hide the cellar entrance to the tunnel?"

Aunt Ann put down her teacup and refilled Mrs. Hubbard's. "I can't think of any reason, unless some later Pingrees weren't proud of having forebears who were smugglers. They might have decided to conceal the evidence and deny the story." She was silent for a moment, thinking. "You say the wall is built of the same stone and mortar as the rest of the cellar? Of course, I know it is for I've seen it many a time myself and never suspected it of being more recent than the other walls. But it can't have been built too many years later or the materials in it would have been different. Only very old buildings have that construction using oyster-shell mortar."

"Would there be any old records or family papers that would tell?" asked Kit.

"If there were, don't you think the tunnel would have been discovered before now?" asked his mother.

"I suppose so. I was just hoping."

Aunt Ann folded her hands in her lap and leaned her fluffy head against the back of her chair. "My grandfather Joseph Pingree used to tell me tales about the house and my ancestors when I was a little girl. That's his father's portrait there over the mantel—another Jonathan. My grandfather had heard them from his father and grandfather who in turn had heard them from his. So they were handed down from one generation to another. That is how I came to know the story of Robert the pirate, and about the children hiding from the Indians in the secret closet."

"It's a shame our grandfather did not write them down," said Mrs. Hubbard.

"I'm not sure but what he did," said Aunt Ann. "He was always being urged to do so, but if he did we never knew about it. He lived on in the house for a time after my father brought my mother there as a bride, but"—she leaned forward clasping her hands together, "my mother wasn't the easiest person to get along with and he moved out for the sake of harmony."

She laughed wryly. "The harmony did not last long. I've hesitated telling you this before, Natalie, but you might as well know, and Abby and Kit also. My mother made our father's life miserable until he got out, too. Things were pleasanter for Jonathan and me then, without the constant friction between them. She was unbalanced mentally and died in an institution. Before she lost her mind completely she told us we must never marry. She explained that there was insanity in her family she had not known about when she married our father. She made us promise her to remain single lest we pass on the taint to any children we might have if we married. It skipped us, fortunately." She sighed deeply. "There! That's off my mind at last."

Abby and Kit were speechless.

Mrs. Hubbard, too, was at first at loss for words. She reached over and placed her hand over Aunt Ann's. "I understand a lot of things now I never did before," she said. "Thank you for telling us."

Aunt Ann smiled up at her. "You wouldn't be here if it hadn't been that way," she said, "so some good came out of it. And I'm glad that our father finally had some happiness out of his life."

Kit reminded her of his question and they welcomed the change of subject. "You said you were not certain but what your grandfather did write things down," he said.

"That was what I was getting at," said Aunt Ann. "By a roundabout way, to be sure! There was an old box of his papers and belongings that I found in the attic when I moved. It must have been put there long ago and forgotten. In any case it was still sealed up as he had left it. I just never have gotten around to open it, but if he did keep any sort of record of the past, it would probably be there. You've given me an incentive now to see what I can find."

"Don't push yourself, Ann, but if you do come across anything that would explain the wall, we'd certainly be interested to hear about it."

She kissed her half sister and prepared to leave. "We'll drive you to church tomorrow and bring you back home with us for dinner afterward."

Abby was last. She gave Aunt Ann a kiss, too, and whispered, "I'm awfully sorry all those sad things happened."

# ❧ 18 ❧

# To Dent the Wall

Mr. Hubbard was already home from the office when they arrived. He was stretched out on a lawn chair enjoying the late afternoon sun.

"You been out gadding?" he asked Mrs. Hubbard as she bent to kiss him.

"We've been to see Ann. Just wait until you hear what the children have to tell you! I'll be back in a moment. I have to start supper."

He looked at them over the top of his spectacles. "What are you going to spring on me now?" he asked. "There's never a dull minute around here. Out with it!"

They sprawled on the grass on either side of his chair and exploded their bombshell. He reacted satisfactorily and was so interested and excited over their discovery he barely scolded them for the risks they had run.

"Take me down to see the tunnel opening," he said, unfolding himself from the chair. "Kit, run and tell Mother where we are going."

"That was a smart idea you had, Pumpkin," he said to Abby as they walked across the lawn. "I suppose no one ever thought of checking the measurements of the cellar and the living room before, because there was never any evidence that a tunnel existed. It's not surprising that the tunnel was brushed off as a legend when no external outlet could ever be found—until now."

Kit caught up with them and they made their way down the treacherous path to the shore. The tide was out, exposing an expanse of seaweed and shell-strewn sand. Gulls and terns took wing at their approach, wheeling and calling their shrill cries.

When they came to the broken-off stone, Mr. Hubbard peered behind it into the tunnel. "I'm not going in," he answered their unspoken question. "And I want you to promise that you'll never go in again, either. I'll get John to help me shove the stone back and we'll find some way to seal the tunnel up forever. We don't want other kids to find this opening and start exploring."

He examined the jagged face of the slanted rock ridge from which the piece had broken off. Then he eyed the slab on the sand. "I've been trying to visualize how it must have looked when it was still part of this rocky ridge," he said. "It must have seemed like a rock outcropping pure and simple, with nothing about it to suggest that it concealed a crevice that led to a tunnel behind it. I can see how the shrubs and roots and foliage must have hidden any suggestion of a passageway."

"But why did it break off *now?*" asked Kit. "There must

have been other storms as bad as this one. Why didn't this happen before?"

"No doubt the other storms all helped," said his father. "They contributed to slow erosion, wearing down the rock and weakening a crack which must have developed over the years. Then, when the thrust and push of this sea came, the time was ripe, and the fault in the stone gave. This piece broke off and fell over on the beach. All of the debris and loose soil and stones which had piled up in the entrance in the course of time were washed out by the ebb and flow of this elemental sea."

Abby turned at the sound of her mother's voice hoo-hooing to them from the top of the bluff. "Mother's calling us. We'd better start back," she said. "Dad, it won't be hard to keep that promise. You couldn't pay me to go in there again!"

"Once was enough for me," agreed Kit. He shivered, remembering.

"All right, I have your word," said their father. They turned and retraced their steps, joining Mrs. Hubbard by the leaning gateposts of the fallen fence.

"Did you ever see such a sunset?" cried Abby, as they reached the top. The west was aglow, pale lemony-green near the horizon while above clouds trailed a glory of crimson and gold across the sky. The west windows of their house flashed back the gold.

During supper they discussed the tunnel, the wall, and Aunt Ann's revelation about the past. They felt deep sympathy for her. "It's tragic, whatever way you look at it," said Mrs. Hubbard. "Ann was so matter-of-fact about it I guess we should be, too. And it was dear of her to point out that some good came of it, otherwise we wouldn't be here. I'm glad she feels that way."

"Poor Aunt Ann, never to have a husband or children," said Abby.

"I hope she finds something in that old box of her grand-father's that will explain why that second wall was built," said Kit.

"And I hope she's looking tonight and that she'll have something to tell us when she comes for dinner tomorrow. I want to find out what's behind that wall—if there's any-thing beside the door." Abby looked at her father intently to see how he would react to this.

Mr. Hubbard helped Kit to another serving of spaghetti and meatballs.

"I'm consumed with curiosity myself," he said. "I wonder how much of a job it would be to break through. We wouldn't have to take down the whole wall, just make a big enough hole to get inside."

"You could get John to help you," said Kit—"that is providing the police don't want him before then."

"True," said his father, "which makes me think we shouldn't delay. You say that you and Abby are driving Aunt Ann to church tomorrow, Natalie? That will leave John free to help Kit and me see what sort of dent we can make in the wall."

"Fine," said Mrs. Hubbard. "But that reminds me. I forgot to let John know he won't be needed to drive Aunt Ann tomorrow. You go tell him before he and Essie leave for the movies. This is the night they always go."

Kit went with his father to John's and Essie's house. They were dressed in their good clothes about to take off. Later Kit reported to Abby that Essie actually looked quite presentable and was more friendly than she had been. They both had been amazed to learn about the tunnel and John had said he would be glad to help close up the entrance and break down the wall.

# ❧ 19 ❧

# A Gruesome Discovery

ABBY WAS UNABLE to keep her mind on the sermon that Sunday morning. Outwardly she looked like a properly reverent young girl, white-gloved hands folded in the lap of her lavender linen jumper, eyes straight ahead, fair hair gleaming. But inwardly her mind seethed.

She hadn't wanted to come to church. She would have much rather stayed behind with Kit and do whatever he was doing. John had appeared just as they finished breakfast, bringing with him a couple of crowbars and a pickax. Dad had said they would close the tunnel opening first. Instead of going with them, she had had to stay behind and help Mommy set the table for Sunday dinner. By now they must have finished with the tunnel and would be in the cellar. She could hardly wait for church to be over to learn what they had discovered.

The only words of the minister's prayer that penetrated her wandering mind was a mention of the hurricane when he gave thanks that lives were spared. She thought guiltily that she and Kit should give thanks, too, that their lives had been spared in the tunnel.

Aunt Ann sat between Abby and Mrs. Hubbard, primly erect in a printed blue and white silk dress, a white net cap holding her fluffy hair. She had been carrying a small parcel wrapped in brown paper when they picked her up at her apartment. Now it rested on her lap for she had not wanted to leave it in the car. She told them she had spent last evening going through the old box of papers belonging to her grandfather and had found something of interest. But she would not tell them any more. There hadn't been time, in any case, before they arrived at Thetford's dignified white church with its slender spire facing on the town's elm-shaded green.

Abby rose with the rest of the congregation to sing the stirring words of the final hymn:

> "Eternal Father, strong to save,
> Whose arm doth bind the restless wave,
> Who bidd'st the mighty ocean deep
> Its own appointed limits keep:
> Oh hear us when we cry to Thee
> For those in peril on the sea."

She sang wholeheartedly, thinking of all those who had been in peril on the sea during the hurricane.

At last came the benediction, silent prayer, and the slow walk up the aisle to shake hands with the minister. Abby said good morning to him but she could not honestly tell him she had enjoyed his sermon.

Once they were outside and out of earshot Abby exploded. "That was the longest, absolutely the longest church I ever sat through!" she said.

"Sh-h-h," whispered her mother.

"I don't care, Mommy. It was! I was wondering the whole time what was happening at home."

She helped Aunt Ann into the seat next to Mother and slid in beside her. Miss Pingree patted her knee. "It was good preaching, Abby, even if you did not hear it. But I can understand how hard it was to keep your mind on it. I'm anxious to know what's been happening myself."

Mr. Hubbard and John and Kit had gone to the beach immediately after breakfast. John examined the tunnel entrance and then turned to Kit. "You must have had some bad moments in there, boy, with the tide coming in and you not able to get out. I told you the tide was on its way in, remember? But little I thought you'd be exploring a tunnel no one knew for sure was there."

With much huffing and puffing the two men pried the stone upright with their crowbars and eased it across the tunnel opening. This would effectively block it until they found a more permanent way to do so.

They finished this chore just about the time Abby and Mrs. Hubbard were leaving the house. Then they turned their attention to the cellar. John went first to the barn for some more tools, a sledgehammer, two chisels and an iron spike. He also brought an electric hand lantern with a reflector to enlarge its beam of light. Mr. Hubbard found a hundred-watt bulb to put in the ceiling light socket.

"From the location of the tunnel entrance on the shore,

I would guess that the door into the cellar should be about here," said Mr. Hubbard, indicating the far right section of the wall. "Let's start here anyhow."

Kit held the electric lantern so the beam fell on the area they had chosen, while John and his father in turn attacked the hard old mortar with the pickax at a spot about three feet up from the floor. Dust from the mortar filled the air, settled on their clothes, and tickled their noses. They shouted to each other over the din, and then tried chipping at the mortar with their chisels, attempting to loosen a large stone embedded in the wall. Bits of mortar crumbled and fell until finally there was a deep enough dent to insert the spike and try using the sledgehammer. John paused to get his breath and to brush the dust from his eyelashes. Then he whammed the sledgehammer against the spike again and again.

"That's getting it!" shouted Mr. Hubbard. "Try on the other side now."

John pounded some more. Gradually the stone moved. One hard blow on the stone itself sent it crashing inward onto the cellar floor with a loud thump. The hole it left was too small to give access, but a good beginning.

They worked with renewed vigor, chipping and hammering until a second stone fell out, leaving an opening big enough to admit a small person. "I guess you're elected, Kit," said his father. "But wait until some fresher air has a chance to get in there. I don't like the smell of it."

Kit did not like it either. The air emerging from the hole was cold and rank and musty, coming from a place where no light or freshness had been able to penetrate for nobody knew how many years.

After several minutes' wait his father said, "I think it will be okay now. Hold the lantern close to your chest and I'll boost you up."

Kit went in feet first. As his toes felt and found the floor on the other side, they pushed the fallen stone away and he slid the rest of himself in.

Seconds passed. Then they heard a frightened gasp.

"What is it? Do you see the door?" Mr. Hubbard called into the hole.

At the same moment footsteps sounded overhead. Abby and Aunt Ann and Mrs. Hubbard came down the cellar stairs. They were in time to see Kit's face appear in the hole in the wall. He was very white, his eyes staring.

He pushed the lantern out in front of him. "Help me out of here!" he cried. "I saw it all right. But I saw something else, something awful. There's a skeleton sitting on the floor just inside the door."

"A skeleton!" said Abby, horrified. Aunt Ann tottered and almost fell, but Mrs. Hubbard caught her in time. Mr. Hubbard grabbed Kit by the shoulders and heaved him into the cellar. Kit was shaking and trembling.

"Put your head down if you feel faint," his father told him. "And everybody try to keep calm. I'm going to have a look." He took the lantern from Kit and thrust his head through the hole, aiming the beam of light inside.

In a few moments he withdrew his head, looking somewhat shaken himself. "Kit is absolutely right," he said. "The bleached bones of a skeleton are resting against a door of heavy timbers, just like the door Abby and Kit described from the other side."

There was appalled silence. Finally Abby asked in a shaky voice the questions in all of their minds, "Whose bones?"

The color had returned to Kit's face; the shock of the gruesome discovery had worn off. Now curiosity was uppermost. "Whoever he was, he must have been there for years and years and years," he said. "He didn't know the wall had been built and for some reason, once he got inside the door, he couldn't get out again."

Abby's eyes brimmed with tears. "It's so awful—to think of him dying all alone in there in the dark."

"Natalie," said Mr. Hubbard. "I think you had better take Ann and the children upstairs. This is no place for squeamish people. John and I will have to enlarge the hole so we can get inside and learn what we can. Put off dinner for a while, please."

They went willingly. There was no protest from Kit about a delay in dinner. For once, he wasn't hungry.

## ❧ 20 ❧

## "Whose Bones?"

MRS. HUBBARD BROUGHT Aunt Ann a cup of strong tea to revive her. In the library where they were sitting the thud of the pickax and sledgehammer came to them muffled, but the noise finally ceased.

Miss Pingree sipped the tea. "I feel better now," she said. "Hand me my parcel, Abby. We might as well have a look at it while we are waiting. It will give us something else to think about."

She untied the string and slid something out of the paper. It was an ancient-looking composition or day book. The writing on the pages was faded and the paper was yellow with age, ragged at the edges. "This was my grandfather's," she said. "See," she opened to the title page, "he printed here: *Joseph Pingree's Personal Book—Family An-*

*ecdotes and Memories.* I didn't try to read all of it. The writing was too hard on my eyes and it was too late at night when I found it in the very bottom of the box."

"What else was in the box?" asked Kit.

"Old letters and accounts and business ledgers chiefly. But this is what I was hoping to find. He tells in it the history of the family as far as he knows it. And I think he gives a clue about who was responsible for the wall. I'm not going to attempt to read from it now. But I'll give you the gist of what I found out. He tells about the first Pingree's acquiring the land from the Indians and building the original house. The first Jonathan was a shipbuilder as we know, but he says that he outfitted privateers. He said there were rumors that he indulged in some smuggling himself and that a tunnel led from the shore to the cellar of the house though it had never been found.

"The part that interested me was the marriage in 1717 of his oldest son, also named Jonathan, to a young woman from Rhode Island, Mercy Philpotts, who was a member of the Society of Friends. According to Grandfather she had excessively strict views of right and wrong and was strong-willed. She wouldn't have approved of smuggling. I suspect it was she who insisted on the wall."

"That sounds plausible," said Mrs. Hubbard. "She may have fussed at her husband until he built the wall to keep her quiet!" She arose from her chair. "I must go to the kitchen and mash the potatoes. The roast beef is done, but I have to make the gravy and put on the peas. Then everything will be ready when Paul is. Excuse me, please."

As she left the room Abby asked, "May I see the book, Aunt Ann?"

"Yes, child, but be gentle with it. The pages are brittle."

Abby took the book and opened it, turning to the first page after the title. She found the writing difficult but she made out the opening sentence and read it aloud slowly. *"I, Joseph Pingree, in the year of our Lord 1880, in my sixty-eighth year, fearing that what I have learned about the history of my family over the years may be lost unless I record same, do herewith begin to inscribe the stories handed down by my forebears and what other facts I have been able to ascertain."*

"Phew! that's some beginning," said Abby, handing the book back to Aunt Ann. "I'd never be able to wade through the whole book in his writing. Does he tell anything about Robert the pirate?"

"Yes, further on he tells the story I've already told you about Robert. If it's the last thing I do, I mean to copy in legible script all that my grandfather has written here and then I shall have it typed and have copies made for your mother and you and Kit. And I believe I'll give one to the Historical Society, too." Aunt Ann's cheeks were flushed and her eyes sparkled at the prospect.

"I wonder if we'll ever know who belongs to the bones," said Kit. "He would have to be a smuggler or a sailor from one of Jonathan Pingree's ships. He must have been someone who knew about the tunnel."

"That's obvious," said Abby, "or he wouldn't have been there! Do you realize, Kit, that our bones might have been found some day on the other side of that door if we hadn't managed to get out of the tunnel when we did?" she shuddered at the thought. "I wish we knew who he was."

Mr. Hubbard had come up the stairs, stepping so lightly they hadn't heard him until he appeared in the hall doorway, dust streaked and filthy. "I think I can tell you, Pumpkin, as soon as I get clean. John and I are through for the time being. I'll be with you in a jiffy."

"Oh, Daddy, how can we wait? We want to know now!" Abby cried.

Kit jumped to his feet. "I'll go get Ma. She'd better turn off the dinner again!"

In less than ten minutes Mr. Hubbard reappeared looking greatly improved. He walked over to Abby and handed her a small object. "That's a bit of whalebone," he said. "Read the initials scratched on it."

Abby studied it intently. "The first looks like an R," she said. "Yes, R. P. It's hard to make them out they are so uneven. After the P there are some wiggly figures—one seven two four. Why that must be a date! 1724!" The significance of the initials finally struck her. "R. P. Robert Pingree! Oh, no! You mean that's who the skeleton is, was?" Tears came to her eyes, but she blinked them back. "Robert Pingree, the pirate, trying to come home."

Her father gave her a moment to recover.

"We found that on the floor of the cellar near his hand bones. Also this." He held out a large brass key. "It must have been the key to the door. That, together with the initials on the whalebone, make me feel sure he was a Pingree. I believe only a member of the family would have had the key. Apparently it unlocks the door from the outside only. John and I tried it in the lock on this side of the wall and it would not turn at all. Which makes me think that there had to be two keys to that door—one in the possession of the elder Jonathan—to open the door from inside. But we can only guess at that."

"What do you think happened?" asked Kit.

"The way I reconstruct things is that Robert escaped

from the pirates or was put ashore here for some reason. He dared not risk being captured by the civil authorities for, remember—Aunt Ann told us there was a law making piracy a crime subject to the death penalty. He must have known about the law for it had been passed long before he went to sea. The best chance he had of not being detected was to make his way up the smugglers' tunnel into his own house. Then he could declare that he had been forced into piracy and safely reveal the name of his pirate captors. His family would protect him against retaliation.

"Once inside the door he must have thought he was safe. Then it shut behind him before, in the dark, he discovered he was trapped by a wall he did not know was there.

"He died of suffocation, I feel certain of that. But while he could still breathe he managed to scratch his initials and the date on this piece of whalebone he probably had in his pocket. His sea bag crumbled to dust when we tried to lift it. It was filled with pieces of eight."

They had been listening spellbound. Abby was the first to speak. "It *was* his ghost I saw! You wouldn't believe me then, but you'll have to believe me now."

Aunt Ann nodded her head. "I didn't know you had seen him, Abby. You didn't tell me. But it is not hard for me to believe that he has been haunting this house, poor lad."

## ❧ 21 ❧

# Grim Problems

THE ROAST BEEF had not suffered by the delay. It was still pink and juicy inside. Mr. Hubbard carved generous slices and helped everyone to fluffy mashed potatoes and gravy while Mrs. Hubbard served the peas and Abby filled the salad plates.

They bowed their heads for grace. "For what we are about to receive we return our thanks to you, Oh Lord," Mr. Hubbard said.

"M-m-m, this is good," said Kit after his first swallow. "For a while I didn't think I could eat, but now I can."

By unspoken agreement no one mentioned the skeleton during the meal. But what they were to do with it was a problem that had to be discussed, afterward.

"He should have a decent burial in the family plot in

Thetford," said Aunt Ann. "That will put his ghost to rest, too, for good and all."

"Do we call the undertaker, or what?" asked Mrs. Hubbard. "I don't know the proper procedure for these things."

"One thing I'm sure of," said Mr. Hubbard. "There will have to be a death certificate signed by a doctor before any undertaker will bury him."

This struck Kit as funny. "You mean a guy who's been dead for over two hundred years still has to have a death certificate? That sounds nutty to me."

"I didn't make the law," said his father mildly. "The problem is to find a doctor. We haven't lived here long enough to have one yet."

"I'll call my doctor," said Aunt Ann. "This would be a good time to catch him in. I'll ring him now, that is if the phone is working."

"I don't know whether it is or not," said Mrs. Hubbard. "But try it and see."

Fortunately it was. Aunt Ann returned from the hall and reported that Dr. Bacon said he would be right over. "I told him it was an emergency," she said, "but he doesn't know what kind!"

Dr. Bacon was a portly gentleman of middle years with a kind face and a hearty manner. He was introduced by Aunt Ann to her new family and then remarked, "You all look mighty healthy to me. What is this emergency?"

"Well, well, well!" he said, after he had been told why he was needed. "I've heard of plenty of skeletons in family closets, but one in the cellar is a new one on me! Take me down, Mr. Hubbard, and I'll have a look."

They were gone for some time. Abby could not imagine what the doctor was doing. He ought to be able to tell at once that Robert was dead just by looking at what was left of him.

Finally the two men came into the room. Dr. Bacon took out his pen and a printed form. "I'm going to put down the cause of death was accidental suffocation," he said. "Poor fellow. He didn't have a chance once that door closed on him. Did you realize he'd lost a leg at the knee? His left one. We found the remains of his wooden leg powdered to dust on the floor." He put away his pen and stood up to go. "This is a strange and fascinating story," he said. "If I were you I would lose no time calling the undertaker and arranging for his final resting place. When this story gets out, as it's bound to, you're going to be bothered by the curious and the morbid."

This was something that had not yet occurred to the family. Dr. Bacon gave the name of an undertaker, told them he was glad to be of service, and left.

Aunt Ann called the pastor of her church to arrange about the burial and Mr. Hubbard talked to the undertaker. By this time Abby and Kit had had enough of all the grim things that had to be done. They did not want to be around when the undertaker came. "Let's get out of here," said Kit. "I want a swim."

They got into their suits. On the way to the beach they met John and told him what had been happening. "When you saw the ghost that time," said Abby, "didn't you say he limped? He did when I saw him, too, and now we know why. He had a wooden leg!"

"He'll not walk anymore," said John. "Once those bones are buried the ghost will be at rest."

It was a warm and lovely afternoon. The water was delicious—cold enough to be invigorating but warm enough to stay in without getting chilled. The sea was calm. They could swim and float and splash without fear of being knocked over by waves. Abby, floating, let herself be lifted and lowered by the slow gentle swells of the sea and felt all of the worry and fear and excitement of the last two days drain away from her.

A shout from Kit brought her head up and she looked where he pointed. A boy and girl in bathing suits were racing down the beach from the cottage colony. Chuck and Patty! Abby and Kit raced to meet them and the four came together in a flurry of sand.

"When did you get back?" asked Abby panting. "You missed the hurricane! And we missed you!"

"I *would* have to be away during all the fireworks!" said Chuck. "Remember I told you this mill pond could kick up a mighty fuss when a northeaster blew!"

"It sure did," said Kit. "Are your houses all right?"

"We got out in time," said Patty. "I wanted so to call you but the phones were dead. We had some water on the floor, but the house held together and Chuck's did, too. My we're glad to be back. Tell us what happened to you."

Abby and Kit looked at each other, the same question in their eyes. Should they tell?

"Lots," Abby said. "We'll tell you some of it if you promise to keep mum. Cross your hearts?"

Mystified, Chuck and Patty solemnly crossed their hearts.

So they were told about the smugglers' tunnel and the skeleton in the cellar. Chuck's and Patty's eyes grew rounder and their mouths opened wider.

"The undertaker's probably been to the house by now," said Kit importantly. "We got out. We'd had enough!"

"Wow, what a story!" said Chuck. "Thanks for letting us in on it. What's your Dad going to do with all those pieces of eight?"

"I suppose he has gathered them up by now and is going to count them," said Kit. "I don't know what will happen to them after that."

"I want to keep the one I found," said Abby. "Kit's been longing for a gold doubloon. If he finds one of them I hope he'll let Kit keep it."

"I should think he would," said Patty. "If it hadn't been for you two none of them would have been found. I hope the next time we come over you'll let us see them."

"Right now I want to see the entrance to the tunnel," said Chuck.

"We'll give you a personally escorted tour," said Kit. "Then we must get back to the house. We want to know what's been happening."

Mother had taken Aunt Ann home by the time they got back. As Kit suspected his father was seated at the dining-room table counting pieces of eight. He had just finished stacking them into piles of twenty when they found him. There were only three gold doubloons.

"With the coin you found in the tunnel, Abby, the count of pieces of eight is five hundred. Now here is something curious. I found a book in the library the other night called *Pirates of the New England Coast.** I just came on it accidentally, but with a pirate in our past I couldn't resist dipping into it. And I stumbled on this curious fact. Pirates mutilated in fighting were given an indemnity—a

* By George Francis Dow and John Henry Edmonds, the Marine Research Society, Salem, Massachusetts, 1923.

payment for their loss of limb or eye or finger. The amounts varied with each loss. But I do remember that the amount for the loss of a leg, a left leg mind you, was five hundred pieces of eight!"

"He hadn't spent the money and was bringing it home!" said Abby.

"What are you going to do with it all?" asked Kit.

"I haven't decided yet. You and Abby are entitled to a gold doubloon each, I should think. I don't know how much the pieces of eight will be worth today. I suppose we can use some of them for the cost of burying Robert. We'll have to think on it."

## 22

# The Racket Revealed

THE NEXT WEEK was one that Abby did not like to remember, although it had its interesting moments. Robert the pirate went to his last resting place in the quiet graveyard in Thetford where his Pingree relatives were buried. Only the family was present. There was no funeral service, just a simple prayer at the graveside, but when Abby heard the final words, "May he rest in peace," she felt a lifting of her heart and a sense of comfort, convinced that Robert had really come home and that his troubled spirit was at rest.

As Dr. Bacon had predicted, the story of the smugglers' tunnel and their grisly find in the cellar leaked out. The telephone rang constantly. Reporters from the local and city newspapers asked for interviews. Photographs were taken of the house, the hole in the cellar wall, the locked door to the tunnel, as well as the blocked-off entrance from the shore. Their friends from Tuppertown called and wrote letters; Mr. Hubbard's business associates asked to come and see where the skeleton had been found. Chuck and Patty and their families came. During this time John had been occupied in repairing the steps to the beach and setting the picket fence and gateposts upright again.

Mr. Hubbard, forewarned, had been forehanded. With a contractor's help, a quantity of concrete had been poured around the stone at the tunnel's mouth, sealing it securely. Robert's skeleton, safely buried, did not have to suffer the indignity of being photographed. The pieces of eight had been put in the bank for safekeeping.

Gradually the furor died down. The story was over and done, quickly supplanted by some new sensation in the daily press. Abby and Kit woke up to the fact that Labor Day was just a week off, and after that they would be starting classes in a new school. They tried to think about it as little as possible.

It is small wonder that their other apprehension about John and the police and the stolen furniture had almost faded from their minds.

One evening about ten days after the discovery of the skeleton, the phone rang. Abby got there first. "Daddy, it's for you," she said disappointedly.

Mr. Hubbard returned to the library wearing a worried frown. "That was Captain Deevers of the State Police. He's coming right over. He wants to tell us what's been happening. I'm afraid John may be in for it."

"Oh, dear," said Mrs. Hubbard, putting down her knitting. In spite of what they suspected, they had all grown fond of John.

Captain Deevers arrived. He had deep-set gray eyes under bushy brows and a cropped mustache on his upper lip. He was lean and athletic looking and when he smiled Abby liked him. "So you are the two young people who helped solve this case," he said. "I am proud to meet you. I hear you've had some interesting things going on here. What I've come to tell you may be a bit of an anticlimax. You seem to have been having more than your share of excitement."

This, Abby considered an understatement.

"What has been happening?" asked Mr. Hubbard. "I have to confess we had sort of forgotten your problem during all of our discoveries here."

"We've made an arrest, several of them," said Captain Deevers, taking the chair Mrs. Hubbard indicated.

"Not John?" Abby asked, anxiously.

"One of my men is taking him into custody right now. We have a lot of questions to ask him. May I tell you what we've discovered, Kit, thanks to your tip about the car license?"

"Go ahead," said Mr. Hubbard. "Fire away."

Abby and Kit were torn between wanting to hear and their fear of what it might mean for John.

"Well, we've been shadowing Folsom, the man you put the finger on, Kit, ever since we identified him as the owner of the car. Last night we caught him and a confederate removing a piece of furniture from a house about fifty miles from here. We arrested them on the spot. It didn't take long for Folsom to talk. He'd been caught red-handed."

"Was John in on it?" asked Abby anxiously.

"No—not this time. His part in the scheme did not come

off. They must have made other arrangements since your house has been so much in the news. But I had better begin at the beginning and tell you what we discovered about the racket."

"Please do," said Mr. Hubbard.

Captain Deevers leaned forward in his chair. "This is how it worked: A decorating firm in Haven City would be commissioned to do over a house or a room in a house. The decorator in charge of the job would persuade his client that a particular antique—a desk or cupboard or highboy or whatever, was the only possible piece to fit the plan for the room. Always at a fancy price, mind you.

"Now this is the clever trick they thought up. The wife of the decorator was sent on every benefit house tour in the surrounding countryside—you know those benefits when the owners of distinguished homes allow them to be viewed by the public who have bought tickets to benefit a hospital or garden club or the like?"

"Yes, I love to go on them," said Mrs. Hubbard. "You get to see houses you might never have a chance to see otherwise."

"Exactly. That's why they are so popular, I suppose. But in this case it was a means of spotting antique furniture which would fill the bill for the decorator. His spotter made notes of what and where. All he had to do was to discover a time when the owner would be absent overnight or for a weekend, then arrange the burglary. The antique would be brought to your old kitchen wing to be hidden until he could have it picked up, then transferred to the van which would be delivering furniture to the client's new home. A very clever racket which has been going on too long."

"How did Folsom get involved?" Mr. Hubbard asked. "He works for an antique dealer I thought you said."

"That was the beauty of it. On the decorator's books each antique was purchased from the dealer, although they were in cahoots. The dealer would arrange the robbery after the decorator tipped him off about what he wanted and where it could be found."

Abby spoke up. "I don't believe John knew about any of it. I think he was just helping out with his truck and that he didn't know the furniture was stolen."

Captain Deevers smiled at her. "I like your feeling of loyalty to him. I must tell you that Folsom did not actually incriminate him. John wasn't in on the real racket. He just grabbed a chance to earn some extra money with his truck, that was all. However, he must have begun to suspect it was not on the level and by that time it was too late for him to refuse the use of your house. But we can't get around the fact that he was hiding stolen goods whether he knew it or not. I promise you we'll give him every chance to clear himself. He must have some pretty good qualities to have gotten you all to stick up for him as you have."

They had to be content with that.

"What a shame all that ingenuity and imagination on the part of the antique dealer and the decorator could not have been put to some legitimate use," mused Mr. Hubbard. "Will the original owners get back their stolen furniture? How will you manage that? And how will the innocent purchasers be paid back for the cash they put out for these things?"

"There are a lot of matters like that to be worked out," said Captain Deevers. "The two masterminds in the racket have already been arrested. We've taken over the books of the decorating firm. From them we hope to trace each piece of furniture to its new owner. Then we can match up this information with our records of burglaries and we should be able to restore each antique to its rightful owner. The people who bought the furniture in good faith will have the amounts they paid refunded from the decorator's assets, even if the business has to be liquidated to provide the funds."

"I can see you have your work cut out for you," said Mrs. Hubbard.

Mr. Hubbard was worried about something else. "This story will make quite a splash in the papers," he said. "I hope you can somehow keep our names out of it- or the fact that this house was used as a hiding place. We've had more publicity than we ever wanted in the last weeks."

"Your names won't appear," the captain assured them as he shook hands all around. "We keep our sources of information to ourselves. We don't want the defense lawyers to know how much we know or how we found it out. You needn't worry about any newspaper stories now. But when the case comes to trial, Abby and Kit will have to testify as witnesses. That is months away. These things move slowly, you know. So my advice is to try to forget all about it until that time comes."

"Well that's a relief, to know we won't be overrun with reporters again," said Mrs. Hubbard. "Thanks for coming to tell us about it. We'll appreciate any consideration you can show John."

"I'd better go along with you," said Mr. Hubbard. "If you're booking John I'd like to arrange bail for him."

"That shouldn't be any problem," said Captain Deevers.

A short time after they left there was a knock on the rear hall door. Mrs. Hubbard opened it to a weeping Essie. "They've taken John away," she sobbed. "I knew he'd get into trouble but he would not listen to me. We did need the cash because we'd gotten into debt and he said it wouldn't do Miss Pingree or you any harm or hurt the house to use that old empty kitchen every now and then to store something in. He didn't know the things were stolen, and when he began to suspect he was in too deep to back out. Now the police have taken him away. Oh, what will I do? What will I do?"

Mrs. Hubbard brought her into the library and made her sit down while she attempted to soothe her. "We believe you. We believe that John didn't realize what he was getting into," and she explained to her some of the ins and outs of the case. "Mr. Hubbard has gone down to the police station with the detective. He's going to arrange bail. Try not to worry."

Somewhat comforted Essie went home.

John was allowed to return with Mr. Hubbard after he told his story at police headquarters and answered questions. Captain Deevers indicated to Mr. Hubbard that his testimony would help convict the criminals when the case came to trial. John himself would have to face charges for his part in the affair. Mr. Hubbard hoped that he might be let off lightly or given a suspended sentence when all the facts were known.

On the way back to Pingree Point, John talked frankly to Mr. Hubbard. "Honest I didn't know I was getting into anything wrong, Sir," he said. "I thought I was just making a bit of needed cash with my pick-up truck, no questions asked. That was my mistake. I see that now. I knew I had no right to use that old kitchen of yours, though I could see no harm in it. I was warned not to talk about it and I was well paid for a few hours work, but I should have asked questions. When I began to smell something fishy, I was scared." He shifted uncomfortably in his seat and spoke with evident embarrassment. "I like working part time for Miss Pingree and doing odd jobs for you, but it isn't like what I used to earn from a full-time job. Then I made the mistake of buying a color TV on time and those payments were hard to keep up. When this chance came along to make some extra money it seemed an easy way to get the cash I needed. I thought of the money first and whether it was right or wrong I put out of my mind. Essie didn't like it. I should have listened to her. I've learned my lesson now. I'll never buy anything again until I have the money saved up to pay for it."

When Mr. Hubbard reported this conversation to the family, they all felt happier about John. They agreed they would keep his trouble from Aunt Ann as long as possible.

# ❧ 23 ❧

# *Pieces of Eight*

THEY TRIED TO put the trial out of their minds for now. Newspapers played up the story of the arrest of a prominent decorator in Haven City as well as the antique dealer and his employee, Folsom. The story of the racket and how it operated was revealed in full. They were relieved to read that their house was referred to as "a long-empty dwelling only recently occupied." Its location was not given or the name of the family living in it.

The owners of the stolen furniture were interviewed as well as many clients of the decorator. The latter expressed horrified amazement to learn how they had been duped. In most cases they showed a complete willingness to see the antiques restored to their former owners. No one, including Aunt Ann, among their friends and acquaintances, suspected the Hubbards of having been involved.

Chuck and Patty might have put two and two together had they remembered the discovery of the shrouded desk that rainy day they had come to play Ping-pong in the ballroom and had explored the kitchen down below—or if they had recalled the lights they thought they had seen in the kitchen wing when the house was empty. But at the time of the Ping-pong game, Kit's conclusion that the desk undoubtedly belonged to Aunt Ann had been plausible enough to make them forget the incident entirely.

The nearness of the first day of school was much on the minds of Abby and Kit. They had driven past the school in Thetford, observed that it was new and modern looking and that it was too far away for them to walk. Abby wished that Patty and Chuck were going to the same school. Instead they attended one in Haven City where they lived most of the year.

The knowledge that their two friends would be coming to the beach many weekends during the fall consoled them a bit. The Burgesses had invited the Hubbards and the Browns to a clambake and lobster feast on Labor Day as a sort of farewell to summer. And Patty had promised to have Abby for a weekend visit later on. So there were nice things to look forward to. Surely she and Kit would make some new friends among the children who lived closer by and went to the Thetford School.

Meanwhile there was the problem of what to do with the pieces of eight.

Mr. Hubbard took samples of the coins to a dealer in Haven City. There he learned that HISPANIARUM ET IND, REX, meant "King of Spain and the Indies" and that coins with that inscription had been minted in the New

World. He told the family this when he came home that afternoon. But his big news was that he had been offered twelve dollars apiece for them.

Abby was stunned. She did some quick mental arithmetic. "Why, if we sell all of them that would be six thousand dollars!" she exclaimed.

"Yes, Pumpkin, and that's a lot of money."

"What will we do with it?" Kit wanted to know.

They had gathered around the kitchen table where Abby was helping her mother shell peas for supper.

Mrs. Hubbard drew her finger down the inside of a pod, spraying the round green peas into the bowl before her. "I've been thinking about the coins," she said. "Abby wanted to keep the piece of eight she found in the tunnel. It would make a nice addition to her silver charm bracelet."

Abby spilled some peas on the floor in her delight at this unexpected suggestion. "Oh, neat!" she cried. "I'd love that. And Kit was hoping for a gold doubloon. Couldn't we let him have one of those? There were three of them."

"That would seem fair to me," said Mr. Hubbard. "Did you know that a doubloon means a double peso? So it is worth double a piece of eight and maybe even more because it's gold. You'll have to keep it in a safe place, Kit."

"There's nothing safer than a safe deposit box, is there?" asked Kit. "Put it there where I can't get at it! But I'll still have the satisfaction of knowing it is mine." He was beaming as he scrambled to retrieve the spilled peas.

"What about the other two? Have you any bright ideas for them?" Mr. Hubbard looked at his wife.

"You guessed it!" said Mrs. Hubbard smiling. "I'd love to have a pair of earrings made of them. Would you mind?

They would be for me to wear now, and for Abby when she's old enough to wear them. Of course I'd have to have my ears pierced. I wouldn't want to risk losing them. But I've planned to do that for a long time anyway. I've just been waiting for earrings that would make it worth while!"

"Oh, Mommy!" Abby's eyes shone. She thought this a marvelous idea. So many girls today were having their ears pierced and she would, too, later on.

Kit and Mr. Hubbard made no objections though they both thought pierced ears rather silly.

"I think Daddy and Aunt Ann and John should each have a piece of eight," said Abby. "For a remembrance."

"Thanks for including me!" said her father. "After we've taken out what we've paid the undertaker and the costs for the concrete, and the repairs of the wall down cellar, we'll still have a lot left," he reminded them.

The kitchen clock ticked loudly in the silence as they thought about this.

Abby nearly upset the peas again in her eagerness to speak. "Robert's grave!" she said. "It ought to have a gravestone on it. Why don't we use some of the leftover money for that?"

They all thought well of this. "It ought to be a simple granite stone, flat on the grave," said Mrs. Hubbard. "With his name and dates and a few lines below explaining that he was captured by pirates but at long last came home."

"Excellent, Natalie, excellent! That's just what we'll do! We must decide what we want on the stone and I'll see to it promptly. I am sure Ann will be pleased with this plan."

Abby wriggled with pleasure. It was such fun spending money in one's mind. "Will there still be some more left after that?" she asked.

Her father grinned at her. "I don't think all of these things will make too big a dent in the amount. Now it's my turn to make a proposal. Your Aunt Ann was talking about having copies made of her Grandfather Pingree's daybook. What would you think of my hunting up a small private hand press and arranging to have a limited edition of the book printed, something well designed, on good paper, with a durable binding that will last?"

"Wonderful! Super! Great!" they agreed.

"A book that we can hand down to our children and our children's children," said Abby looking far into the future.

"And give copies to the local libraries as well as to the Historical Society," said her father.

Kit popped some raw peas in his mouth. "Here, quit that!" said his mother. "There won't be enough for dinner if you eat them now."

He pushed his chair back, moving away from temptation. "We ought to ask Aunt Ann to bring the family history up to date," he said.

"Kit, you're on the beam!" his mother exclaimed. "Of course we should, for we don't want to have the Pingree history end with Grandfather Joseph. I'm sure she'll love doing it and be so pleased that we want her to. But I think you and Abby should write something for the book, too. You should describe in your own words how you discovered the smugglers' tunnel and all that happened afterward, winding up with Robert's skeleton and the laying of the pirate's ghost!"

"Now you're the one who's on the beam!" said Mr. Hubbard.

"Abby'll have to do the writing," said Kit. "I'm no good at that."

Abby was wordless, hugging herself, she was so tickled with this plan. English was her favorite subject; she even had a secret ambition to be an author when she grew up. To be asked to contribute a chapter to Great-Grandfather Pingree's book thrilled her to the core. She hoped she would be able to fulfill their expectations.

"Kit, you're good at math and I'm not," she reminded him. "You can tell me if I leave anything out, anything important. Is it all right if I call Aunt Ann right now and tell her what we've decided? I can hardly wait to hear what she says!"

Aunt Ann thought it the most perfect idea she had heard of in a long time. "What's more," she told Abby, "I've already rented a typewriter and begun to copy the book."

This acted as a spur to Abby. Dinner would not be for an hour yet. She found herself a ruled pad and some sharpened pencils and planted herself in a wicker chair on the side lawn where she could be alone and quiet. How should she begin? She thought about this hard and long. The words Great-Grandfather Pingree had used came back to her, "I, Joseph." She would follow his style. She smoothed the pad and began to write.

Meanwhile, Kit went in search of John. He had been troubled, wondering if John knew the part he, Kit, had played in the arrest of Folsom. He felt that he ought to tell him. He would never feel comfortable with John again unless he did. He hoped that John would still be friends with him after he knew.

He found John puttering in the barn. His manner was perfectly friendly, but Kit did not know how to begin.

"What's on your mind, boy?" John sensed his uneasiness.

"You're fidgety. What excitement are you going to be dreaming up next?"

"I've had enough excitement for a while," said Kit. "But I can't help thinking about the trial. Abby and I are going to have to be witnesses. Did you know that?"

John was surprised. "Can't say that I did. And what will you be witnessing about?"

"About you and Folsom. It's because of us you both got arrested," blurted Kit. "We didn't mean to make trouble for you, John, honest."

John was staring, openmouthed. Kit jabbered on. "We found that desk in the old kitchen and the next time we looked it was gone. That made us wonder, so we kept checking the place. Then we found the corner cupboard, and when Folsom came to get you to help him move it, we hid upstairs in the ballroom and watched. As soon as you drove off with it in your truck I ran outside with my flashlight and got his license number. That's how the police knew and that's when Abby saw the ghost."

"Well, I'm a son-of-a-gun!" said John. "I should have known that not much escapes two curious and bright young-uns like you and Abby." He laughed ruefully. "But I'm glad you found out, Kit. What we were doing was wrong. I did not know how wrong until the police told me what it was all about. I should never have gotten into it and believe me, I'm glad it's over."

A question came to him. "How come you decided I wasn't in on the whole thing, Kit?"

"We thought you were at first. But as Abby and I got to know you we didn't believe that anyone we liked so much could be bad on purpose. Or anyone Aunt Ann had trusted for so long. We were scared when that detective came to arrest you. We hope you won't have to go to jail."

John studied Kit in silence for so long Kit began to be worried. Then he smiled and held out his hand. "Thanks for believing in me, Kit," he said. "If I have to spend a short time in jail I know you and your family will look after Essie. Shake my hand. Let's always be friends."

With a much lighter heart Kit sought out Abby. She was scribbling busily. "How's it going?" he asked.

"I'll read you what I've written so far." She turned back to the first page, revealing many scratched-out lines and corrections. " 'I, Abigail Pingree Hubbard,' " she read, " 'in my twelfth year, and my brother Christopher Woodruff Hubbard, who is ten and who shall hereinafter be referred to as Kit, are great-grandchildren of Joseph Pingree,

author of most of the foregoing portion of this book. On an August Saturday in the year of our Lord nineteen hundred and sixty-five, the day after Hurricane Doris, Kit and I discovered a tunnel used by our ancestor, Jonathan Pingree in the early seventeen hundreds for the purpose of smuggling in goods and contraband from the Indies, in order to avoid paying taxes to Great Britain.' How's that for a beginning?"

"Terrific!" Kit was filled with admiration. "You can sure sling words, Abby."

She was pleased at his praise. She chewed the end of her pencil reflectively while her eyes followed a robin hopping across the lawn. The words must be well and carefully chosen. They must tell her descendents and Kit's exactly what had happened. She must watch her spelling, too.

"Kit, run and get me a dictionary," she said. Then she bent her head over the pad again and resumed writing.